# TOMMY QUINN

## THE WHITE APACHE

Roy Scha...

D1041528

ISBN 978-1-63630-936-1 (Paperback)
ISBN 978-1-63630-937-8 (Digital)

Covenant Books, Inc.
11661 Hwy 707
Murrells Inlet, SC 29576
www.covenantbooks.com

# Dedication

This book is dedicated to my wife, Kathy, who asked me to write her another Western novel with a cattle stampede in it after I had been run over by a herd of cattle and was black and blue from head to foot except my face.

Kathy asked me to write down my spiritual experiences when we first married over forty-six years ago. When I came awake on the operating table in 2018, I realized how close I was to death. I came home and wrote the book of my life's experiences. My wife asked me to write her a Western novel. I didn't think I could. But after her loving pleadings, I sat down and wrote my first Western novel. She wanted it longer, so I wrote a part two and gave it to her, a forty-sixth wedding anniversary present. That day, she said, "What about the next one?" So now you have *Tommy Quinn—The White Apache.*

# CHAPTER ONE

The cactus was blooming with their large yellow blossoms, making the desert smell fresh, and the grass was starting to grow because of the spring rains. There was a light breeze out of the southwest, and the sun was coming up over the ridge in the Texas sky.

The young man was sitting on a ridge, looking down on the cattle being gathered for the trail drive north to Montana. It was April first, and it was Tommy Quinn's twenty-second birthday. At least that was the day he was found and nursed back to health six years ago. It was the day six years ago that he was found on the ground in the middle of a ranch yard where there were a lot of Indians, along with a few white people, lying on the ground dead. He was one of the white people left there for dead, but he was dressed in buckskin clothes and moccasins. They guessed him to be about sixteen years old.

Tommy Quinn had been raised for about ten years by the Apache tribe. He could remember being taken from the wagon when the Apache raided their wagon train. He wasn't sure what happened to his family. He had a brother and two sisters. The cavalry had come upon the wagon train as it was being raided and ran the Apaches off. The chief grabbed Tommy and threw him across the black-and-white pinto horse and took him out of the Texas country. He was raised as one of the chief's younger sons.

He was taught in the ways of the tribal customs of the Apache. He had to learn to speak their language and how to ride horses and take care of the horses. He was taught to think as the Apache and eat and survive as one in the desert. They would take him out and leave him alone in the desert to let him learn to survive with nothing but a knife for a month at a time. It was hard sometimes being treated differently because of his white skin, blue eyes, and blond hair. He learned to fight, and he got where he could handle any of the other young warriors. He could fight with his fist and his hands and his feet equally well, maybe even being deadly. He was good with a knife and a bow. He was taught to use his head and learn to use his judgment in everything he did.

Tommy Quinn had been taken to the Bob Yost ranch, and they nursed his two bullet holes until he was up and going again. He had to learn to talk to the whites again. It came back to him as he listened to the people talking around him. He could remember his little sisters and his brother. The children in the home helped him remember. They worked with him and got him to talk with them. It wasn't that easy, but they wouldn't give up on him, and he enjoyed their company. Sally was about his age and worked on teaching him to read and write. It took several months for him to heal and get back on his feet again.

The Yost family was looked down on when they took the young man in. The neighbors kept telling them that he would kill them in their sleep. Tommy had always been against killing. He could always see in his mind the killing of the people on the wagon train as a child. He would, and had for years, had nightmares of that day. No, he didn't want to be a part of it. The Apache tried to change that. He had had to kill to protect himself several times. It would make him sick each time he did.

Bob would take him out and herd the cattle. He got where he would go out alone and watch the cattle for a week at a time. He would take a small bedroll behind his saddle and live off the land. He had his knife and a canteen. He kept his knife in his sheath that he wore behind his neck on his back. He could pull it and could throw it for thirty feet and hit a target one-inch big.

He loved the cattle and horses. He understood them and could take care of them. Bob would trust him in whatever he did with the cattle. Tommy would keep them on water and good feed. He would protect them at all costs to himself.

*****

As he watched some men gathering the cattle for a trail drive, he noticed a man riding up into the Yost herd. The man on the sorrel horse with one large white spot on the horse's flank was cutting out several of Bob's cattle. Tommy rode down beside the man and said, "These cattle belong to Bob Yost, and you would do well to trail them back to where you got them."

The man pulled his gun, which was his second mistake. The knife was sticking through the man's gun hand and into the man's hip. He pulled his hand up to get it free. That was the third mistake. It sliced through his hand, cutting off his trigger finger and two others. He tried to get the gun out with his other hand. That was his fourth mistake. Tommy came up off his horse and shot through the air from about six feet away. His foot caught the man in the jaw. Tommy landed on his feet and kicked the man in the jaw again. It hung to one side of his face all broken up. The man was out and within five minutes was tied across the thief's horse with the spot. He slapped the horse on the rump and headed him back to the trail drive.

Bill Wilson, the trail boss, had watched the goings-on and rode on down to talk to Tommy and introduced himself. He held up his hand as he rode up. Bill said, "That was pretty fancy, but why did you do it?"

Tommy showed Bill the cattle with the Yost brand and said, "The man pulled his gun, and I did what I had to. He was stealing our cattle, and when he pulled his gun, I took care of it. He knew they were not his cattle. I sent him packing."

Bill said, "I saw the whole thing, and you did what you needed to do. He was one of my men. When I get back to the herd, I will fire him." He then smiled at Tommy and held his hand out and shook Tommy's hand. "I'm taking a thousand head of cattle to Montana. If you want a job, you can have it."

Tommy smiled back and said, "I know cattle some, but I would protect you and your herd and scout for you to Montana."

"I guess I don't understand how someone so young could scout and protect my herd," Bill questioned.

"I can only tell you I can do it. I can handle myself, and if I am not what you want, send me home. You see, I was raised by the Apache from a little boy as the chief's son and was brought into the Yost family when I was left to die. I was shot up, and they saved me. I have lived with them for six years, and they took me in as one of their family and taught me to read and write."

"You have the job, and I will pay you what you are worth to me when we deliver the cattle to Montana," Bill said.

"I will need to go tell my family what I am going to do. I will be along and watch over you and your cattle in a couple of days, Mr. Wilson," Tommy said.

*****

That evening at the supper table, Tommy told Bob and his family what had happened to his cattle and what he had done to the man stealing them. "If you run into a man with three fingers gone, you will recognize the rustler. He also rides a sorrel horse with a large white spot on his left flank. Bill Wilson hired me to go with the cattle drive to Montana. He wants me to scout and protect the men and herd. I will try to be back in the spring, if not before."

Bob took Tommy aside and handed him a 45 Colt and holster and two boxes of shells. "You will want to get good with this and know how to use it. Only use it with good judgment. I don't have any money to help you, but you probably won't need it. Good luck, son. Take that chestnut horse and saddle you've been riding. You have earned him."

He got up and walked to the barn to get on his way. Sally was waiting for him when he walked in. She talked to him and told him he meant a lot to her. Just before he headed out of the barn, Sally walked up to him and threw her arms around his neck and placed her lips on his. She held there for a couple of minutes, and then when she turned loose, she said, "I love you, Tommy Quinn. You come back to me." He nodded, smiled, and walked out.

# CHAPTER TWO

Riding to catch up with the herd, Tommy noticed a group of men camped along the creek. The sun was going down over the western skyline. Clouds were building, and it was going to be dark tonight. He noticed the sorrel with the white spot.

He rode back up the creek where he had seen some sage grouse and worked his way up within thirty feet. He took his knife, and it shot out. He dressed the bird and started a small fire out of sight. Then he ate his meal.

He then rode back down close to the camp of the men and put his moccasins on. He worked up within earshot of the men and listened. They were planning on taking over the herd in two nights. They planned to sneak in on the camp and kill the men and take over the herd. He overheard them say, "Wadez will be there, and he will let us know if there is anything wrong. He will be watching for us and let us know if Wilson suspects anything."

Tommy studied the men and the camp. He noticed how they arranged the sleeping of the men. He noticed that the men didn't keep a night watch. They brought their horses in on a rope line tied between two trees for the night. They had plenty of whiskey to settle them down for the night. Tommy moved back and watched until they were all bedded down. He rode up over the ridge where he would be out of sight and went to sleep until just before daylight.

\*\*\*\*\*

Bill sat, having a cup of coffee. The others were eating their pancakes and some bacon. They had their horses saddled, and when it broke daylight, they would have the cattle on the move north. The night riders came in and rode up to the fire and stepped down to get their breakfast and a cup of coffee. There was a little frost on the grass this morning. Three other riders had ridden out around the south end of the herd. A few of the cattle had gotten out of their beds and started looking for the green grass.

Bill looked out into the dark and then over to the western sky, wondering if Tommy Quinn was going to really come. It had been several days since he had been hired. What kind of scout was he? How could this young man protect him and his herd? He probably was just a kid, and he had seen the last of him. But then again, he had sure handled that cattle rustler that worked for him. Bill had fired him and hired Con Wadez to replace him. Things always worked out. Con showed up just when he needed him the next day. He seemed to be a good hand, and he was glad he had shown up when he did.

Bill looked at the sky and the breaking of dawn and shouted, "Let's get out there and head them out. Cookie, get the wagon headed out. We will see you about noon. Have some coffee and some lunch for us. We will see you then."

Noon came with the sun bearing down on them. It was really nice to have it shining and no rain for a day or two. The temperature was mild, and the cows moved along just smoothly. Bill looked up to the west and noticed a lone rider sitting on the ridge, watching. He had been there for a couple of hours, watching the goings-on of the men and cattle. Who was he? Was it an Indian or just trouble? At lunch, he was there drinking his coffee and watching the west skyline, wondering where the man had gone.

He heard someone standing behind him say, "Bill, could I talk to you? We need to talk. I will ride along with you when we head out. I would like a job if you're still hiring."

Bill jumped and turned to look to see who was talking. Tommy sat down beside him and put a finger to his lips. Bill looked curiously at him said, "Are looking for a job, boy?"

Tommy looked at him and said, "Looks like you are ready to head out. How about I ride alongside you for awhile and we will talk about the job. I will go get my horse, and we will get on our way where we can talk. We can figure out if I can go to work."

An hour later, Tommy rode up beside Bill and told him thanks for not giving away who he was. "Have you got a man named Con Wadez working for you now?"

Bill answered, "I hired a man whose first name is Con, but that isn't the last name he goes by. I hired him a day after I fired that rustler you put over his saddle. What about him?"

"His name is Con Wadez, and he is a part of the ten men following you about eight miles back. The leader of the gang is the man I put on the horse and you fired. Tomorrow night, they plan on raiding your camp and killing you all. They said that Con would be their lookout for them and signal if all wasn't right."

Bill asked, "Just how do you know all this?"

"I sat and listened to their plans last evening. You need to have Con on night watch this evening till midnight. He will go on a long ride with me for about eighty miles west of here. He will help me along with the ten horses that we will be delivering to the Navajo over in New Mexico. He will not want to return when we get there."

Bill asked, "Why is that?"

"Because he would have to walk and he will not have his horse. I will give all the gang's horses of the men that are following you to the Navajo. I will be wearing my moccasins when I take their horses tonight and leave for New Mexico to the Navajo. Those moccasin tracks will show the Navajo took their horses. You will need to watch tonight, and if tomorrow the gang heads for you, they will be afoot. They might try to come after you. Move the cows as far as you can tonight and leave before daylight if you can. Keep a lookout on your back side for a few days. I will be back," Tommy promised.

Bill waved goodbye and kept the cows moving. Con rode up beside the trail boss and asked what the kid wanted. "He wanted a job, but he has no experience. I don't need some wet-nosed kid I have to babysit. I sent him back to his mammy."

Con smiled, then turned, and rode off.

*****

Tommy Quinn killed himself a rabbit and made himself some supper. He took another nap and would wait until late tonight to go in by the cattle. In the meantime, he watched the night watch ride out to the herd. He studied Con as he rode. He then noticed him going south toward the gang's camp. Tommy headed south and got ahead of him. He would wait for him to show up.

Two miles from the camp, he waited along the trail behind some willows. As the horse and rider came along, the lariat settled over Con's body and jerked him off his horse. His horse stopped and looked back while Tommy kicked Con in the head. He grabbed the gun and belt and searched him for a knife. There was one in his boot. He then caught the horse and took the rifle and scabbard and put it on his horse. He tied Con with rawhide strings and took the neck scarf off the man and gagged him. He threw him over the horse and tied him down.

He headed south but stayed away from the creek. In another five miles, he noticed a light ahead. He then circled around the camp and went south another mile. Tying the horse to a tree with the rider across the saddle, he checked the man and made sure he was secure. He rode back about a half mile and put his moccasins on.

He walked toward the fire and stopping every few feet to make sure there were no lookouts. They had set their camp up the same as the night before. The horses this night were a couple of hundred feet further south of camp. He sat and studied the horses and watched their ears. No one was watching, and the men seemed to be happy, passing the bottle around. It was all right to just be lazy. Anyway, every day Bill and his crew ate the dust behind those cows. It was another day they didn't have to eat the dust.

Tommy slipped back to the horses and started tying each lead rope to the next one's tail. He had all ten horses head and tailed and led them to his horse. Jumping astride his mount, he headed south to get Con and his horse. Con's horse nickered as he rode up. Con was awake and trying to get loose. Tommy checked the ropes and readjusted the gag. He tied the ten horses to Con's horse's tail. He then took the horse with the man on it and headed out with all eleven horses in a line and headed west.

After a day's riding, it was getting dark when they came upon a creek. He saw a turkey in a tree. He took his knife, and with one movement of his arm, the turkey lay on the ground. Con had watched him knock the turkey out of the tree at thirty feet with a knife put in the turkey's head.

Tommy slid Con off his horse and laid him up beside an oak tree. In an hour, the turkey was done. He untied Cons hands and gave him a drink after removing the gag. Con started to cuss at him, but he was told he best keep quiet. It would be hard to eat with the gag in his mouth. Handing him the leg, Tommy stepped over and cut the breast off the bird for himself and ate it.

Tommy then tied a rope to Con's arm and untied Con's feet. Con was allowed to go down by the bushes and then down by the creek to wash. When done, he brought him back and tied the feet together and the arms around behind the tree. The horses had been led into the creek for a drink earlier and tied out on picket and allowed to graze some. His horse, he picketed out by itself.

Before daylight, he and Con ate some more turkey. Con was on the saddle with hands tied to the saddle horn. His legs tied under the horse.

It would be a few more days to the Navajo camp. When Con found out where they were headed, fear struck his eyes. He and his gang had raided these Navajo camps and stolen horses and took their women and abused them. He had reason to have fear showing in his eyes.

# CHAPTER THREE

Bill had gone back with five of his men and watched the outlaw's camp. The men at the camp were just sitting around and looking at the tracks of their horses and looking at the moccasin tracks. They weren't sure whether to follow the horses or head for the trail drive. They made their next mistake. They decided to head for the cattle drive.

They came up the hill. They knew Con Wadez would be in their camp and would surprise them. Halfway up the hill, Bill put a bullet at their feet. They all hit the ground. One of the men got up looking to where the shot had come from. He took another step, and Bill put a bullet in his boot top. He was down, screaming. They started shooting at the top of the hill. When they stood up and again started up the hill, all six men shot for the outlaws' boot tops. Four more went down. The other five that were left stood up, holding their guns over their heads. They then gave them a throw. They reached down and took the other men's guns and belts off and threw them up the hill. They went over to the five down men and helped them up and started back down the hill.

Bill had two of his men bring up their horses. With their rifles across their laps, they rode down and talked to the gang. They asked Bill why they had done this to them. They hadn't done anything. Bill looked at the man with the missing finger and said, "I told you, if I ever saw you again, I would shoot you. I guess losing those fingers wasn't enough. Looks like you will not have a leg. Someone must have shot it off. Why are you walking anyway?"

One of the gang members said, "Some Indian came into our camp and stole our horses."

Bill said, "Like Con said, you were going to kill us and steal our herd. I was good to him and let him take night watch and leave the country. You had better head south, and if I ever see any of you again, I'll not shoot so low. Next time, it will be between the eyes. We will take your guns so you can't use them. Don't come back!"

Bill turned and took their guns with him and headed back over the hill. He left two of his men to watch until evening just to make sure they weren't following.

A few days later, they had the herd fifty miles further north, and all was going well.

*****

Tommy Quinn had ridden for eighty miles and found that he had to travel another twenty. The desert country had some tall red cliffs along the valley. Con begged him to not take him to the Navajo camp. Tommy had asked him several times what made him so scared of the Navajo.

Con, showing fear more every day and begging him more to turn him loose, asked again, "You just can't take me into the valley. They will kill me."

"Are you just that much of a coward and afraid they will hurt you? You wanted to face Bill Wilson and his crew. What's so different about these people? Start talking," Tommy ordered.

Con screamed, "They will kill me because of what our gang did to some of their women and little girls. We did things to them I'm not proud of, and then we killed some of them. I didn't mind killing them because they were red."

"You deserve to die. Maybe over an anthill or in a rattlesnake pit—maybe over a slow fire. I have seen men die like that a lot of times. I have no use for men like you. You see, I was raised by an Apache chief. I lived with them in my growing-up years. I have seen the worst of the ways that they torture men. I should leave it up to them," Tommy said.

After riding a few more miles, Tommy got off his horse and untied Con. He jerked Con off his horse then cut the ropes off Con's feet and hands. He looked at Con and asked, "Do you know where California is? I suggest that you go see it. If I ever hear of you or see you again, I will tie you to your horse and take you to the Apache. They know how to make a slow death last a few days. The Navajo would just kill you."

Tommy was watching the men along the top of the hills as he rode along. He waved at them. They knew he had seen them, even though they were well hidden. He broke over the hill and down into the valley. Several warriors rode up beside him. He held his hand up in friendship. He then spoke to them and told them he needed to talk to their chief.

When he was riding into the camp, the chief walked up to him. He handed the lead rope and the eleven horses to him and said, "I come in peace. I bring horses back that were stolen. I go back to where I come from."

The chief held up a hand and asked him to get down. He said, "You are a warrior and need to prove yourself. You fight our mighty one. You win, then you go."

Tommy got down and walked to the fire and picked up a piece of meat cooking there. One of the women there yelled a scream and pointed at him. She had been stolen from the Apache camps years ago. She was the Apache chief's daughter. She said, "This is my brother. He is one of the Apache chief's sons. Do not fight him. He will hurt your mighty one. He might kill him."

The mighty one walked up and laughed, "She scared for her brother. Bring him on. We fight with knives, and he kills me, he goes home."

She said to the mighty one, "You ever hear of Tommy Quinn. This is the Apache Tommy Quinn."

"I heard he died in the raid on a ranch in Texas. You lie," he said.

Tommy said, "I am Tommy Quinn. I will fight so you can defend your honor. I come as a friend, and I will leave as a friend."

The mighty one backed off about thirty feet and made a run at Tommy. Tommy jumped into the air and kicked the knife from his hand, and the second kick hit his head and put him down. Tommy stood back and watched until the big man got up. Tommy let him walk over and get his knife. He had fear starting to show in his eyes.

Tommy asked, "You ready to die or walk away?"

He started at Tommy. Tommy reached up behind his neck, pulled the knife, and threw in into the mighty one's heart. He stopped and looked at Tommy and fell forward. Tommy walked over, pulled his knife, and wiped it on the big man. He put it away and mounted his horse.

He raised his hand to the chief and then to the girl. Turning, he rode away. Tommy Quinn headed back to the trail drive.

# CHAPTER FOUR

Bob Yost headed into the town to get supplies. There was a young man on a horse heading east. When he rode up, Bob raised his hand. He looked at the young man who looked somewhat familiar. He introduced himself as Billy Quinn.

Bob said in surprise, "Would you be related to Tommy Quinn?"

With a large smile, Billy said, "My brother. If you know Tommy, then he must still be alive. Tell me about him."

"Jump down and tie that horse to the back of the wagon, and we will talk on the way to town. Tommy was found all shot up about six years ago in a barnyard west of here. He had two bullet holes in him. Nobody wanted anything to do with him because he was riding with a bunch of Apache as the chief's son. He was dressed in buckskins and moccasins. I decided to take him in, and my wife and kids nursed him back to health the next few months. He was raised by the Apache and as chief's son for I guess ten years."

Billy asked, "Where is he now? I'd sure like to see him. I was four years old, and he was six when I last saw him the day the cavalry rescued the wagon train. I'm twenty now, so Tommy's twenty-two."

Bob smiled at him and said, "I guess we figured pretty close. His birthday wouldn't happen to be April first? He took off to Montana on a cattle drive. He was going to be their scout, and he said he was to protect the men and cattle."

"His birthday is on April 6. How is he going to be good enough to protect a bunch of men, a herd of cattle, and be a scout to Montana when he has never been there?" asked Billy.

"You have to remember he was raised by the Apache as a warrior. He took off here and never had anything but a canteen and a knife. I gave him a gun, but I'm not sure he'll ever use it. Some men showed up here, saying an Indian stole ten head of their horses and headed for New Mexico. I believe that Indian was probably named Tommy Quinn. Five of them all had their legs shot up. That was probably Bill Wilson, the trail boss."

"How do I go about finding him? Ma and Pa wanted me to find him. He has two sisters that would like to see him," Billy said.

"I'll tell you what, he promised Sally he would be back in the spring at the latest. If you went wandering around from here to Montana looking for him, you would probably get lost, and he would beat you back here anyway. When we get into town, you write your family a letter, and we can let them know he is alive."

Billy told how the Quinn family had traveled on to Tucson, Arizona. They had started up a small trading post and built it up over the years to having supplies shipped in and was tied in with Billy's uncle that would freight the supplies in and had other wagons to deliver them to other small towns and the ranches around the area. Billy had decided to go see if he could find his long-lost brother. If he was alive, he would find him. He was just glad he wasn't with the Apache anymore.

As their wagon went up the street to the Abilene Trading Post, several men sat in front of the saloon on the bench. Four of them sat there with legs wrapped up. Two of those men had no lower leg. There was one of the men with only part of his fingers. Bob recognized him as being the one Tommy had cut the fingers off in a fight.

That one called into the saloon and called out some men. Two men came out and stood and watched the wagon go by. The men talked for a moment and started down the street, following the wagon.

The Deputy US Marshal Don Noon was standing in his office and watching the street. He had been watching this group of troublemakers for about a month. He stepped outside and walked slowly down the street to where the two walked. He knew the Yost family and the young man they took in. The talk had been all over the country. The young man had lived with the Apache and was white.

When the two followed Yost into the trading post, the marshal slipped around back and came in the back door. He stood behind a row of shelves, listening. He recognized trouble when he saw it.

Bob had asked the clerk for a pencil and paper. He also asked for an envelope. He told Billy to go sit at a table and write a letter. Bob continued on gathering up the supplies he needed. The larger of the two men walked up and ran into Bob, knocking him down with the sack of flour landing on top of Bob.

The man said, "Well, mister, I guess I didn't see you walking there."

Bob turned over and went to get up. The other man walked up and kicked Bob in the ribs.

The second man said, "I guess we just don't like Indian lovers. You know the ones that take them in and let them live with their wife and girls. Your Indian over there must have learned to write. I guess we will have to teach him a lesson on fighting also. Your boy there cut our friends fingers off a month back. Maybe he will need a little trimming also."

The marshal stepped out from behind the shelves. "You're both under arrest for disturbing the peace. Start walking to the jail. Walk out onto the street and you can drop your belts and guns."

As he walked by, he gave Bob a hand up. Noon said, "I'll be back, and let's talk."

Noon followed the two men out onto the street. They were turned facing him with their hands hung low over their guns. He looked at them and said, "You want to try me? Go ahead. I can either put a bullet between both your eyes or blow the legs out from under you like your buddies down the street. Looks like they made a bad choice. You decide, and I'll oblige. Your choice."

They looked at each other and dropped their gun belts on the ground.

One looked at Noon's badge and realized he had made the right choice then said, "You're that Don Noon, the Texas Ranger that has that reputation."

Don nodded. Their faces turned white, and they turned for the jail.

Deputy Noon walked back over to the trading post. He walked in and introduced himself to Bob and Billy. After explaining to the marshal who Billy was, he told of the story of Tommy Quinn. Don told Bob that he would keep the men in jail for a week and let them pay a hefty fine. He would then stay on their tail and watch them for a while—just keep a watch over your shoulder out at the ranch.

Bob asked, "How did it come that four men all got their legs shot up? Looks like two of them lost their legs, and the other two crippled up."

Noon said, "They all came into town all shot up. They said one man shot in the leg bled to death, and the other four were crippled. There were five more with them. The one down in front of the saloon has a couple of fingers cut off. Funny thing is they caught a ride with some rancher in a wagon, and not one of them had a gun with them. I asked them what had happened to them and if I needed to go after the one's that shot them up. The one with the fingers cut off said it was that Indian boy that you have living with you. None of the rest really could come up with a good story among themselves."

Bob said, "I'll tell you what Tommy Quinn told me. The man missing fingers was rustling some of my cows when he was caught. He approached him, and the man went to draw his gun. Tommy threw his knife, and it went through his hand and stuck in his hip. The man jerked his hand up and sliced off his fingers. He then tried to reach over with his left. Tommy said he jumped into the air and kicked the man in the jaw, knocking him off his horse. They both landed on the ground with Tommy landing on his feet, and the man continued to go after his gun. Tommy kicked him again and laid him out. He tied him across his horse and sent the horse packing. Tommy said Bill Wilson, the trail boss, had watched him and then took the man to the cow camp and was going to fire him. Bill hired Tommy to be a scout and watch over the crew and the cattle on their way to Montana. Tommy came home and let me know what he was doing. I gave him a belt and 45 Colt with a couple of boxes of shells. I'm not so sure he will learn to use it. I didn't have any money to give him, but he said that was all right. He just takes a canteen and his knife and goes out and survives weeks at a time. I guess that is what he gets being raised as an Apache."

"Sounds like an amazing young man. You say Billy or his family hasn't seen Tommy for sixteen years. That is going to be quite a reunion. I look forward to meeting him," Don said.

Billy said, "I will too. I sure want to get to know him. Bob said he should be back from Montana by spring."

After going to the post office, they headed for the ranch. It was after dark when they pulled up to the house to unload the supplies.

Sally came out and saw Tommy and gave him a hug. That is when she realized this was a stranger. She stepped back all embarrassed and wasn't sure what to say. She finally came up with "Who are you? I thought you were Tommy."

Her dad covered for him, "Sally, this is Billy Quinn, Tommy's brother. Billy, this is my daughter, Sally Yost."

Billy said, "Hello! I'm not sure whether I should shake your hand or get another one of those special hugs. I guess that one was for Tommy." He reached over and gave her a hug. "That one's for Billy. Let's get this wagon unloaded before I get into any more trouble."

Supper was a fun time getting to know each other. They all wanted to know about the Quinn family. Billy was even more interested to learn of Tommy and his life. He had never really got to know Tommy. He was only four years old when Tommy was taken from the family. For all they knew, Tommy was dead.

# CHAPTER FIVE

Bill Wilson watched the back trail and the skyline constantly. The ten men didn't show up, and neither did Tommy Quinn. He was beginning to think something had happened to Tommy. They were coming to the Red River. Where would they be crossing? It was known for its quicksand and flash floods.

Tommy had passed the herd several days back. He needed to be up ahead and see what dangers and other things that would affect the herd. He came to the large river. People he talked to called it the Red River. He rode up and down it for several miles. He had seen where wagons had crossed it. He rode into it and found the bottom to be solid for a half mile stretch.

He had been studying the birds and the animals. The night sky had had a haze building around the moon last night. It was dark, and he had seen a few warriors moving to the north twice. They were hunting parties. Something was going on. He would have to check it out. He had something much more important that needed to be done tonight.

He headed south to find Bill and get things taken care of to keep the cattle and the cowboys alive. He rode until he couldn't see. An hour before the eastern sky had yellow streaks in it, he was heading south again. Later that day, he saw the cloud of dust in the sky. He continued to watch the animals and their behavior. He pushed on a little faster with the urgency he felt inside.

It was noon when he rode into the camp, and the men had come in for their coffee and some stew. They were letting the herd water in a creek and get some rest and a bite to eat. He walked up behind Bill and said, "Looks like everyone is getting a rest. It's time to head north."

Bill jumped and looked behind him. "You always have to walk in and scare me! I have been watching for you for a week now. What is your hurry to get the cattle on the move so fast? The sky has been clear for a week, and it is hot. The cattle need rest."

"Tomorrow early, a large rainstorm will hit west of here. Later tomorrow, it will hit here, and you will not cross the Red River. If caught in the river, the cattle and you will die. Sand in the bottom of the river changes, and cattle will get caught in the sand and die. I found the one crossing where cattle can cross by tomorrow evening and live. You wait longer and you will have to wait a week or two after this storm before crossing."

Bill asked, "Why do you know this? How can you know this rain is coming?"

"I studied the animals and birds and the night sky for days now. The Apache ways tell me it is coming. You need to push the cattle hard and be across the river, or you will not cross for maybe two weeks. Then you will have to find a new safe place to cross."

Bill looked at Tommy and said, "You are sure of this, aren't you? It will be hard on the cattle, and they will get very tired."

Tommy said, "Cattle can rest when they are across the river. It will be very muddy and hard to walk for a few days. They can eat grass and rest then go on."

"You need to get something to eat so we can go on," Bill said.

Tommy said, "No time to eat, we move now and trail late tonight. Tomorrow, you need to push hard to beat the rain. I will eat tonight. Tomorrow, after we are across the river, I need to go look into the trouble that is building in the north and take care of it for you. Let's get the cattle moving now!"

Bill had hired this kid, and here he was telling him to move the herd in the heat of the day and wear them out. He studied him for a minute and stood up and yelled, "Round them up and move them out."

Tommy told Bill, "I know where the good solid bottom is at. It is the only place in several miles that the cattle will not sink. I will get into the lead of the herd. I will be out front a half mile. Just follow." He got on his horse and headed north.

Bill just shook his head and watched the Apache kid lead them on. Why did he trust him so much? He just sat on his horse and wondered. He trusted him with ten men. The boy had taken the ten horses and Con Wadez, and there was never a glimpse or a word of his doing it. But it was done.

Tommy rode out in the lead and had found a rabbit and had killed it and taken the time to cook it and eat it. When Bill came past the spot where the fire had been, he saw the rabbit skin and bones. He had to smile and think how this was a boy he would like for a son.

The cattle were tired when it got dark that night. Tommy rode into the camp and walked over to Bill. He said, "I didn't scare you tonight." The men were eating the stew Cookie had made for them. They looked at Tommy and wondered why he was here.

Tommy told Bill to get him a couple of sacks, and he would ride ahead when they got close to the river and put them on a stick to flag the crossing. He told Bill to make sure the cattle crossed only between the flags. On either side, he would lose cattle.

Bill asked him if he was hungry. He nodded and walked over to the fire and dished up some of the stew. He took two biscuits and went over and sat on the ground cross-legged. The men studied him as he ate. Some of them had seen the rabbit bones and wondered how he had gotten him without a shot. He didn't even wear a gun. That was strange in this country.

The next morning, the moon was full and working its way to the west horizon. It had a ring around it. He got up and walked over to Cookie and told him he had started the fire. "We need to eat, and when it breaks light, we need to have the cattle heading north."

Tommy said, "Cookie, you get out in the front of the herd and follow me. I will get two flour sacks and mark the crossing for you. You need to be across the river a little after noon. Go out about a mile and find a high spot. When the floodwaters hit, you don't want to be caught in them. Make sure and stay in the middle between the flags. That is where the bottom is most solid." Tommy helped Cookie get the breakfast for the hands and rousted the men out.

Bill said, "You are sure in a hurry this morning. You trying to take over my job as trail boss."

"You get the cattle over the river and let them water on the other side or as they cross. The floodwaters will hit and wash them away if they are not across just after the sun is straight up." Tommy then walked over and saddled his horse and got the flour sacks from Cookie. He rode around the cattle and started them moving north. The night watch headed in to get a bite to eat. A half hour later, the crew was moving the cattle north, and the sky was breaking daylight.

Bill looked at the sky and shook his head—not a cloud anywhere. His thoughts he said out loud, "I must be crazy listening to that kid." Four hours later, he noticed clouds building in the western sky. He then rode up through the men and told them to push a little harder—maybe not as crazy as it appeared in the western sky. It was turning black.

Tommy was waiting at the river and led Cookie across. He waved him on and started back across. He rode up to the man leading the drive. He pointed out the flags, and each took a position by a flag. Another man rode down, and Tommy had him lead the cattle across. They continued across with the last cattle rushing down to the river for a drink.

Tommy rode up to Bill and said, "Get them on across and now. I hear it coming. We are going to get caught in it."

Bill said, "The sun is still shining."

Tommy looked at him and said, "Can't you hear it coming? Take your gun and fire it into the air. Get them across now."

Bill pulled his gun and shot twice into the air. The herd started to move. He rode along the rear of the herd and had the men shoot several times. The cattle couldn't stampede but were moving on across. They were tired but moved on across. As they were coming out the other side, the river started to rise. It came up a couple of feet. Then they heard the rolling water coming, and they got after the cattle. When up about a quarter of a mile, the water was still moving up behind the cattle. They moved on up, letting the cattle graze. They were tired and hungry. The men let them spread out and went to the chuck wagon to get some coffee and wait for Cookie to finish the stew over the fire.

Tommy rode up to Bill and said, "Thanks for believing in me. I have to get going to see what the trouble we have brewing is going to do. I will see you in a couple of days. I have no time to talk. This is important."

A couple of the cowboys walked over and brought Bill some coffee and stew. Watching the boy ride away, they asked Bill, "Who is that young man? One of the guys were rumoring that he was someone running with the Apaches and got shot up. It is said that some rancher took him in and saved his life."

"That, my friends, is the best decision I ever made. I watched him take on a man rustling cattle. The man drew his gun. That young man stopped him and knocked the man off his horse and then tied him across his saddle. You remember I fired a man when we were first starting. You remember Con I hired? He was one of the gang we shot up. He took Con off night guard and then rode south. You remember that group had no horses. He took the horses and Con to the Navajo in New Mexico. He scouted and knew where to cross the river. He saved the herd and probably most of our lives. He was raised by the Apache chief as his son. He is the best thing that ever happened to all of us."

# CHAPTER SIX

Letting the two men out of jail, US Deputy Don Noon had been watching the four crippled men. They seemed not to be healing all that well. Two were barely getting around. The other two that had only one leg needed help getting around. There were four others that seemed to just be waiting around, looking for trouble to start. Three weeks had passed, and they were getting on each other's nerves.

Don had walked out one day, and the men were all watching him. Two of them had their horses tied in front of the saloon. Those two got on their horses and headed toward the Yost ranch.

After watching them ride out of town, he went to his stable and saddled his horse. He led him to the café and picked up a sandwich. He was twenty minutes behind the two troublemakers.

Going to the top of the hill, the two watched the house for some time. Noon sat back on the next hill, watching them. Billy came out of the barn, leading his horse. He headed east to check the cattle on the east pasture. The two worked their way around and followed Billy. Once he was out of sight of the house, the two moved in on him. They split up so they could come in from opposite sides of Billy.

Billy looked up and saw the men coming. Recognizing the men, he turned toward the house and took off. The two cut him off by riding up beside him. Grabbing his reins, they pulled him to a stop. They ordered him off his horse. They hit him in the side and then in the head. "We are going to teach you how to be an Apache, Indian lover. You cut the fingers off our friend, and we are sure you had something to do with our buddies all getting their legs shot off."

The larger of the two pulled his knife and held it up. "I'll show you what Apaches do with these." Billy kicked him in the knee as he walked closer. He held the knife again and went for Billy. When the knife hand was over his head, a bullet went through the palm of his hand. He looked down at his hand and noticed two of his fingers were gone.

The other man turned and pulled his gun to look who had shot. He made his second mistake of the day. His gun went flying, and he had a hole through his hand. "Men, I want to tell you something. This man knows nothing about Apaches. It's his brother that lived and was raised as the Apache chief's son. You wouldn't have ridden up on him like you did Billy here. The last man that pulled a gun on him lost part of his hand, as you well know. Billy, get the men's guns, and I'll take these men back to jail. This time, I'm going to charge them with attempted murder."

"I thank you, Deputy Noon. I guess I will have to watch closer next time," Billy said.

"Can you get those two ropes off their saddles? Put a loop over each of their necks and tie a knot so they won't get them off. Would you take the two horses back to the ranch, along with their guns? I'll be out in a day or two and get them. These men will have less energy by the time we get to town."

The two started to object when the ropes went tight with a jerk. One of them fell and was dragged for five feet. "I'll drag you clear to town. Now get walking. We should be there by dark. If you walk fast, the café might just be open, and I can get you some supper," Noon stated. He pulled his sandwiches out and ate them while they were going.

Noon walked into the saloon to see how things were going. He saw the man with the missing fingers. He walked over to the table he was sitting at and kicked the chair out from under him. He looked down on him and said, "The next time you and your buddies try to go murder a man, I will take the other hand off and maybe the other leg. Would you like to tell me why someone took your horses and somebody shot your legs off? Start talking and now."

The man on the floor reached for Noon's leg. When his hand hit the floor, Noon's heel slammed down on the hand. The sound of the fingers breaking was loud enough, so the others in the room could hear. "You are under arrest. I won't lock you up tonight. You reached for my leg, and that is an assault on a law officer. Your two buddies you sent to kill a man today are in my jail arrested for attempted murder. You will be charged for sending them out to do it and being a part of it."

*****

A few days later, Con Wadez had found a horse and came riding into town. He noticed the men sitting in front of the saloon on the catwalk. He nodded at them as he rode down to the stable. After putting his horse away, he walked back up the street to the café. He ordered some lunch and looked around. One of the gang members that saw him ride in, came in, and sat beside him.

Con asked, "Is that young man that is a friend of the Indians in town? I'm going to find him and kill him. He stole all your horses and took me to the Navajo camp in New Mexico. He turned me loose just before we rode into the Navajo camp. You know the one we stole the horses and Indian girls from. He turned me loose and told me to head to California, and if he saw me again, he would tie me to my horse again. Then he would haul me into the Indian camp and turn me over to them. Actually, he said Apache camp. Nobody orders Con Wadez where to go. What happened to all the gang, Sam? It looks like they all ran into the Army."

"All of our horses were stolen by the Indians and left us afoot. We decided to go after the trail crew and their horses. They were waiting as we walked up the hill. They knew we were in trouble and didn't have our horses," said Sam.

Con said, "That young man that took me to the Navajo camp had all your horses. He gave the horses to them. He said he was raised by the Apache as the chief's son. We need to find him and kill him. Where are the rest of the guys?"

Sam said, "One of the men bled to death, and four of them got shot in the legs by Bill Wilson's cowboys. Three are in jail held for attempted murder. That leaves Matt, Ray, and me."

"Where does that leave us?" Con asked.

Sam answered, "I believe that Tommy Quinn went with the trail boss, Bill Wilson, up north. I think that US deputy marshal is going to ride out to the Yost ranch and bring in some horses in the morning. If we were to get the men out of that jail when he was gone, we just might get away and follow those cattle up north. It would be a pleasure to kill Bill Wilson and his bunch. I personally want to torture that Tommy Quinn."

Noon had two men watch the jail while he was gone. He was on his way out to the Yost ranch by seven. He didn't like the looks of the new man around town. Him hanging around that worthless bunch didn't look good. He had an early breakfast and took some jerky with him for lunch. Leaving town wasn't good, but he had told Bob Yost he would be there to pick up the horses.

*****

Two men watched outside the stable. One watched the jail, and the other two went into the stable. Con got his horse and saddled him. The stable owner went over to get paid. While he was watching the man get his money out of his saddlebag, the other man hit the stable owner on the head. They tied him up. The other men came in and got four more horses. They led them down the alley behind the jail. Two men held the horses while Con walked around the front and walked in. The two men inside looked up as Con walked in.

"Could we help you? The marshal is gone and will be back this evening," said the deputies.

Con pulled his gun and told the men to drop their belts and guns. "Now go. Let those men out of the jail, and you take their places. Don't do anything stupid. We will leave the one that can't walk to make sure you don't make a lot of noise. He can play sheriff for a while. You be good, and he won't have to kill you."

They all walked out and around back. Everything went well, and they all headed toward the Yost ranch. Con asked, "What's that US deputy marshal's name anyway?"

Sam said, "His name is Don Noon."

Con jerked his horse to a stop and shouted, "The Don Noon that was the famous Texas Ranger. He has faced several men with their guns drawn, and they all died before even one got off a shot. We better just head for the cattle drive and leave Don Noon and Texas behind."

Sam asked, "You scared?"

Con was shaking and yelled back, "Dang right I'm scared! You should be too! Let's head north!"

A week later, the five men were in northern Texas. They were within a few miles of the border and the Red River.

# CHAPTER SEVEN

Tommy Quinn studied the tracks of the two hunting parties he had seen heading north. He had followed them for several days. While sitting by a large brush next to the creek, he saw movement several miles away. He sat for several hours when he noticed that the movement was heading south toward him. He could not put his mind on what it was.

He realized there were two groups of men and horses. There were three in one group and four in the other. The three went down in a draw. They were following the four. He rode down closer and noticed the four were Indian braves in a hunting party. He stopped and tied his horse in the draw several hundred yards from the three. Working his way up to the three, he listened to what was being said. They were white and had been working their way toward the four. The three were busy watching the Indians.

He worked down the draw from the three and untied their horses. Walking slowly and softly, he took them back to his mount. Head and tailed, he led them around and out of gunshot range. He got close to the four and let out a coyote cry. The four pulled up and looked to see where the sound came from. They knew it was an Indian and not a coyote making the call.

He rode slowly toward the four until they noticed him. They rode toward him. Stopping a way off, they saw he was white. Tommy continued to walk slowly, leading the three horses. He held his hand up in a peace sign. They came in around him and rode up to him, noticing he had no gun. There was no knife in sight also. He started to speak to them. He asked if they were hunting food or men.

They had seen no men. They had seen very little to kill for food. He asked if they would like to have the three horses he was leading. There were smiles on their faces. They asked where he had found them. He told of the three men waiting to ambush them in the draw ahead. "This was their horses. Take me to your village, and I would like to talk to your chief."

They turned and headed back the way the four had come. Tommy held up his hand and motioned for all to stop. He rode a few steps. He reached up, and his hand swept out his knife, and it stopped a rabbit. He got off and picked it up, handing it to one of the party. At that moment, another jumped out, and instantly, Tommy had him. Tommy walked over and got the second rabbit and skinned both. Walking over to some brush, he picked up some dry brush and lit it. In half an hour, they were all eating.

By dusk, they rode down along a creek bottom to several tepees. The four of the hunting party had told the chief what Tommy had done to save their lives and fed them. The chief wanted to know where Tommy had learned to speak the Apache language so well.

Tommy told them that he was raised as an Apache as the chief's son. He also told the chief of the three men that sat in ambush of his warriors. "They have no horses and will have to walk out of this desert."

Tommy explained that a herd of cattle coming north in a few days would come across the reservation land that belonged to the Indians. He studied the number of women and children in the camp. "We will give you five cows for letting us cross your land. You move west about ten miles and wait for the herd. I will cut out five of them for you. This will feed your people for a few months. We will give paper to show you own the cows and not steal them. No one can say you steal white man's cattle. You will agree to not bother our cattle and keep others from stealing any cattle also."

The chief said, "If we protect you, we should have seven head."

Tommy agreed to that and said, "I will ride back and see what white men do. If they come toward your camp, I will let you know."

It was after dark that Tommy saw the light in the distance. The men had been following the Indians. He worked his way toward the camp and found it was the three white Indian hunters. They had one man out away sitting behind a bush as a night guard. Tommy watched for a while and then worked his way to the man. The man was half dozing when a foot clubbed him in the head. Tommy took the belt and gun and tied the man with his shirt.

Tommy sat down and waited to see what was going to happen. The second man came to relieve the guard. He whistled before he came in to the first. Tommy whistled back. The man came, walking up to the first. Tommy jumped, and his foot hit the man's jaw. The second foot hit the side of his head at the ear. He was down and tied. His gun and belt were no longer with him.

Tommy worked his way in by the fire. The third was sitting against the creek bank, drinking coffee with his back toward Tommy. Tommy just walked in, and the man asked, "How is it going out there?"

He answered in his Apache language, "Really good."

The man jumped up and started to turn when Tommy's foot hit him in the back of the head. The man fell forward and tried to get up. The second foot hit him in the temple. He was out. Tommy didn't take time to tie him. He just gathered the belt and guns. He found the rifles and gathered them up also.

After getting back to his horse, he headed back to the village. He waited until it was light and rode in. The chief met him with several of the braves that he had ridden in with yesterday. He told them the men were following the horse tracks toward their village. He said, "I don't think they will come this way without their guns. I had my moccasins on. They will know the Indians have their guns. I will ride back by and see which way they are going. They will probably get hungry with no guns."

Tommy was sitting on a ridge, watching the cattle strung out going north. All seemed to be going well. That evening, Tommy walked up and sat down beside Bill. He looked up and jumped, spilling his coffee. "Why do you always do that?"

Tommy sat and smiled back at him.

Bill said, "Why didn't one of you men say something?"

None of the men said anything. Finally, one of them said, "That is what you get for hiring an Apache, Boss."

Tommy got up and walked over and got a plate of ham and beans with some corn bread and honey. He walked back over and sat down on the ground and said, "Pays pretty good. This is my second meal with you, Boss. Have you had any trouble lately?"

Bill shook his head in the negative then said, "We are going into the reservation lands, and I hope we don't lose any cattle or men."

"You will lose seven head of cattle to the Indians. They will move their village along the trail. We will give them a bill of sale for the cattle. With this, they will let us cross their lands and also go along and help protect us. They need that many cattle to feed their wives and children for the next few months," Tommy said.

"Why can we trust them?" one of the men asked.

"Because I saved four of their braves from an ambush. They are Apache, and they are my friends. The three white men that tried to ambush them no longer have any horses. When I came back, they were heading for the Indian Village. Now they have no handguns or rifles. The Apache have them. We need to watch for them and make sure and not have anything to do with the three whites. They will steal our horses and guns if they have a chance."

Bill nodded his head. "We will give up seven head. That sounds like a bargain if they also watch and guard us."

"I will ride and watch the ones that are following us. I will talk to you in a couple of days," Tommy said.

The sun was bright, and there was a breeze out of the northwest. The grass was growing, but it was getting hot during the middle of the day. Tommy had ridden several miles south and was sitting under a large brush with a lot of shade. He could see for miles, and all was good. No trouble was in plain sight. It wasn't the plain sight that he worried about. It was the trouble that was hiding in the dark corners of life.

He would have to go north to keep an eye on the three whites. There was the trouble that was always just looking them in the eye, and you didn't even have to look for it.

Two days later, he was sitting on a ridge, watching three men working their way south. They were hungry and worn out. He changed into his riding boots. He rode down by them and started to talk to them.

He asked, "Where are your horses? I don't see a gun between the whole bunch of you."

One of them said, "Some Apaches stole our horses and our guns. There were four of them all in a raiding party. They all came in and beat us up. Then they took our horses and guns."

Tommy asked, "If you had guns, how did they get in on you? I guess I will have to watch and be really careful. They didn't get my horse when I saw them."

"They must have gotten your gun. You don't have it."

Tommy was watching the three as they talked. One of them kept catching the eye of the one that was talking. Tommy could see what was about to take place. They couldn't. Just as the man got behind Tommy, Tommy pinched the horse's neck below the mane. The horse struck out with both hind feet several times. It caught the man in the stomach twice and in the head once. Tommy turned the horse around and did it again. Both men were kicked and down.

"I guess that will help you get your heads on straight. You had better head southeast toward Weatherford. If I see any of you again, I'll stake you out on an anthill in the sun and let them eat your eyes out. I'm riding on southwest of here. Don't follow," Tommy demanded.

# CHAPTER EIGHT

Five men were following the cattle trail. Con said, "We can't be more than two days behind the herd. We will shoot that Bill Wilson and his cowboys up. We will take their horses and make them crawl all the way to Abilene, Texas. They don't have any idea we are anywhere in the country."

Tommy Quinn was lying on his stomach, listening to the threats against Bill Wilson and his crew. It was a dark night with no moonlight. The moon would be late tonight.

Con said, "Tomorrow night, we had better start putting out a night watch. We will get a good night's sleep." They passed the bottle around one more time.

Laughing, Matt said, lifting the bottle high over his head, "To that Apache that steals horses, may we hang him from the highest tree."

Con laughed with a roar. "Maybe he will take me to the Apaches so I can laugh in their faces. Pass that bottle around another time. Matter of fact, open another one. Tonight, we celebrate."

Tommy Quinn moved back from the camp. Walking up the creek to where their horses were tied, he tied them head and tail. Their saddles were in a pile against the tree. Tommy took his knife and cut all the cinches and the leather straps that held them. It was about a half mile to his horse. He headed for the cow camp.

He walked in next to Bill and shook him. Bill jumped and then looked up. "What's going on, Tommy?"

"I have five horses that belong to that same gang you shot up. Con Wadez is leading them. They are back about two miles. They were mostly drunk, celebrating your death and mine. If they wake up and notice their horses are gone, they might come before light. You best be on the ridge above their camp and make sure they turn back. I will go see the one who follows them. He may catch up with them tomorrow sometime."

Bill asked, "What should I do with the horses?"

"Depending on what happens tomorrow. I might give them to the Apache."

\*\*\*\*\*

Tommy rode off the hill to meet the man following the gang. He hailed the man as they rode toward each other. Tommy noticed the US deputy marshal badge on the vest. It had the name of Don Noon stamped on it. The deputy noticed Tommy had no gun.

Noon smiled and asked, "Are you Tommy Quinn by chance? I've heard a lot about you."

Tommy smiled and said, "I am. What can I do for you?"

The deputy smiled and said, "I'm looking for five men that I need to arrest. Two of them broke jail, and the others helped them."

Smiling, Tommy said, "If we hurry, we can catch up with them before they get their legs shot off them like their buddies did back by Abilene. What were the two in jail for?"

"Attempted murder of a young man about your age named, Billy Quinn."

Tommy jerked his horse to a stop and asked, "What did you say?"

"Your younger brother that came looking for you. He's staying at the Bob Yost ranch until you get back next spring. Let's go get these men before they ride away."

Tommy said, "They won't ride anywhere. I took their horses up to Bill Wilson, and he was going come back to make sure that they didn't follow like they did the last time. Last time, Bill gave them a warning shot, and they just kept coming."

"So that is what happened to all the men without legs in Abilene. If they didn't learn their lesson the last time, they had better get smart real fast."

\*\*\*\*\*

Bill and his crew watched as Con and his gang came walking up the hill. Bill drew his rifle and put a shot at Con's feet. Con looked up and could see no one.

Don Noon shot and kicked up dust behind Con. The men weren't sure what to do. The four had been in the slaughter of Bill Wilson before. Three of them and Con threw their guns to the ground and raised their hands. The other turned to shoot at Don. Noon's bullet hit him between the eyes and the second in the left shirt pocket.

Bill walked down to the men and helped pick up the guns.

"Where are your horses," asked the deputy.

"Some Indian stole them. We saw the moccasin tracks. He cut up all our saddles," Matt said.

Bill said, "Why did you come back? Maybe we needed to shoot all your legs out from under you. Tommy, I guess you had better go find their horses. It's going to be a long walk back to Abilene without their horses. If the deputy takes you back and you return, the only warning shot will be the one through your head next time."

Deputy Noon said, "Those horses were stolen horses. Do you have any idea where they went?" Noon gave Tommy a wink.

Tommy said, "I'll go round them up for you. They will need them for evidence. Horse stealing is a hanging offense. I think I saw them up north of here."

When he returned with the horses, the deputy sat down with Tommy and told him about his brother. He said that his sisters and parents were all alive and lived in Arizona.

# CHAPTER NINE

Three men had gotten a ride into Weatherford several days later. They went to the US marshal's office. He was out of town for a couple of days but would be back any time. They headed for the saloon to get a drink. It was what they needed on an empty stomach. They did get a sandwich but kept on drinking.

The next morning, they were at the marshal's office. Sam Kapper walked in and was telling the deputy how the Apache had taken their horses and guns. "There were four of them. They jumped us and beat us up. Then they stole our horses and guns. They then ran their horses over us. We hadn't done anything to make them want to hurt us."

US Deputy Marshal Mark Adams looked at them and asked, "What were you doing on the reservation?"

"We were just riding north, and they came and attacked us," Kapper said. "We need to get our horses from those horse thieves."

"I don't really have time to ride there. I have to go check on another matter up that way. Get yourselves some horses, and we will leave first daylight in the morning," the deputy said.

The deputy went to the telegraph office and wired the US marshal's office in Dallas. He sent the names of the three men and wanted to know what was known about them.

His reply that evening said that they were known for causing trouble with the Indians. They were suspected of hunting down several Indians and scalping them. There were no charges on them, but they bore watching. He was told to watch his back side.

It took several days to get to the area where they had lost their horses. They followed the cattle drive for a couple of days.

Sam Kapper was always talking about how bad the Indians were. He said, "I'll bet that we will find that they have stolen cattle from the cattle drive. You can see that the whole tribe is following the herd."

When watching the place, the village had camped where they could see that there had been a cow butchered. Sam pointed it out to Deputy Adams. The deputy was getting nervous about the way the three men were talking about getting even with the warriors.

Coming up on the village, Deputy Adams started to ride around the camp. The deputy wanted to talk to the trail boss about the butchered cow. The three men wanted to ride in and make an example of the Indians and see if their horses were there.

Deputy Adams said, "Are you all nuts? The four of us and twenty of them don't look like too good of odds. We will go talk to the trail boss. They have been following him, and he will let us know what has been happening."

The herd was a couple of days ahead of them.

*****

Tommy rode up to Bill Wilson and said, "We will be off the reservation tomorrow. I have ridden ahead, and there is no trouble ahead of us. There is trouble following two days behind us. Three men come with a marshal. They talk of causing trouble with Indians over their horses, along with the cow they had killed."

"Can you take care of it, or should I ride back with you?" Bill asked.

"I took care of them once, and I can do it again. There are six warriors wanting to cut the other six head of cattle off and take them back to their village. You make me out a bill of sale, and we can go cut off the six slowest cattle that are dragging behind. One is a little lame but will travel back to their village all right."

Tommy enjoyed talking with the six as they headed the cattle back. The village would be moving toward them and meeting them on the creek a few miles back. He had known two of the warriors from when he lived with the Apache as a young man.

*****

Tommy had ridden ahead and met the deputy and the three with him. They could see the six Indians trailing the six cows. As Tommy rode up to the deputy, he noticed the looks on the three men with him.

The deputy held his hand up and introduced himself as US Deputy Mark Adams.

Tommy introduced himself as Tommy Quinn.

The deputy asked if he was part of the Indians trailing the cattle behind him.

Tommy answered, "I am."

Sam yelled out and said, "These are the Indians that stole our horses and guns! They are stealing those cattle now! Let's take care of them now!"

Mark yelled at the men, "You just shut your mouths and let me find out what is going on here."

Tommy said, "These men own these cattle. I have a bill of sale for seven head of cows made out to them." He handed the paper to Deputy Adams with Bill Wilson's name on it. "You can ride up the trail a little way and talk to the trail boss, Bill Wilson, if you want."

He looked at the paper and nodded his head and said, "I guess that this will take care of the cattle. There is a matter of the horses they claim that the Indians stole and their guns."

"You will want to know that these men were following four braves that were out hunting for their village. This was on Indian lands. They were hidden down in a draw, ready to ambush the four braves. They were planning on killing them for their scalps. I listened to them and turned their horses loose. The next day, they continued on to kill the Indians. I went into their camp and took their guns away from them and gave them to the Indians. I came back and sent them to Weatherford, Texas."

"Were you alone?" asked Adams.

"Yes. When I talked to them, they tried to steal my horse. They didn't get it done," Tommy said. "If you don't believe me, you have them take off their guns, and they can take me on. All three at once. They will confess when I'm through with them. Have them get off their horses, and we will have their trial here."

The three looked at each other, grinning, and Sam said, "You have to get off that kicking idiot of a horse you're riding."

Tommy asked, "Have you had reason to be afraid of him. Maybe the last time we met." Tommy stepped down from his horse and invited them to do the same.

Deputy Adams said, "Drop your guns, men. I don't think this is fair, but if this young man thinks it is, go ahead."

Tommy smiled and said, "Fair to whom."

With the guns dropped, the three surrounded Tommy. Sam took the first swing at the young man, only finding a foot kicking him in the throat. He lay on the ground, trying to get his breath. At the same instant, Tommy jumped and swirled with a kick in the next man's mouth. The third went to turn and run but was too late. He started to run when a foot in the middle of his back doubled him over, and he lay, screaming. His back was broken.

"Deputy Adams, why don't you take these men back south and give them to Deputy Noon to put with the rest of his crippled up no goods?" Tommy Quinn said.

Then it hit the deputy. He knew he had heard the name Tommy Quinn, the Apache kid, in a telegraph a few days ago. Adams got off his horse and walked over and took his hand. "I know Deputy Don Noon very well. He has saved my life over twenty times as a Texas Ranger. Help me get this bunch tied on their horses, and I will put them in jail where they belong."

Tommy looked around and saw the six braves sitting and watching. Tommy looked around at Deputy Adams and waved goodbye. He headed toward the cattle, and they were on their way to their Indian village.

Tommy stayed there for a day. He taught the braves how to fight with their feet like he had learned.

Back to the job he was hired to do, he left there being friends.

# CHAPTER TEN

M el Wadez sat on his horse, watching the Yost ranch house. He had camped there for the night. Billy and Sally came walking out of the house. They headed for the barn. Sally went into the barn and got two halters. Back to the corral, they stood and talked for a few minutes.

Billy asked, "Which horse do you want to ride today?"

Sally looked the horses over and said, "I'll take the one with the four white stockings. He is my favorite. He is a good rope horse if we need to pull any cattle out of a mudhole. I've actually gotten to where I can rope calves and doctor them if I need to." She called him, and he came to her.

Wadez kept a watch on them while they saddled and went to the house to get their lunches. He had a lot of patience. He wanted to get to the young man that put his brother in jail. He followed them when they left the ranch house and watched as they rode to the range.

The two were in the middle of dragging a yearling heifer out of the mud. There had not been enough rain to keep water in the pond. The mud hadn't been cleaned out of the pond for several years.

Sally had her rope around the heifer and pulling on her. Billy had already thrown his rope over the whole body, so it settled down around the legs. When Sally started pulling, Billy pulled, and the rope closed in around all four legs. It pulled the legs up in a bunch, pulling them out of the mud. Sally's horse jumped ahead as she kicked her horse. The heifer flopped over and came sliding out of the pond through the mud. Sally jumped off her horse and pulled her rope off the neck of the heifer. When Billy let the slack to his rope, the heifer got up and wandered off to the herd that was watching.

Mel Wadez rode up with his gun drawn. "You two seem to make a good team. You must be Sally Yost, and you, young man, must be that Apache kid I hear so much about?"

Sally replied, "I'm Sally Yost, but this is not Tommy Quinn. This is Billy Quinn, his brother. Yes, Tommy was raised by the Apaches, but he is not an Apache. Who are you? Why the gun?"

"I'm Mel Wadez. It is my understanding that this Apache kid helped arrest my brother. I understand he took him to the Navajo camp and was going to turn him over to them but turned him loose. He then helped turn him over to the Marshal Noon, and they now have him in jail. They want to try him for murder."

Billy said, "I know nothing about him doing these things. I haven't seen my brother for over sixteen years."

Sally came back with "I only know that Tommy came back to the ranch one evening and said that he was going to go with the trail drive to Montana. He took his horse and hurried off to catch the trail drive. I sure don't know anything about this other stuff you're telling us. It sounds a little far-fetched."

"The only thing is I don't believe you. So just head up that trail there to the north and don't try anything. I would use this gun. And that's not so far-fetched."

Sally asked, "Where are you taking us?"

"We are going to get my brother out of jail first of all. Then we are going to see if you are lying about this, not being the Apache kid. I really don't believe that he hasn't seen his brother for sixteen years. That is more than a little far-fetched."

"How are we going to get your brother out of jail?" Sally asked.

"You are going to go hide while I see if that US Deputy Marshal would like to let my brother go. He either lets him go, or you die," Wadez said.

Down in a creek bottom along some willows, Wadez tied them to a big tree and took their horses on up the creek. He headed for town.

He walked out of the ally and up to the two men sitting by the saloon. Both men were crippled, and each had only one leg. Wadez sat down beside them and asked, "Do you two know Con Wadez?"

Both looked at him and nodded their heads and asked, "Why would you like to know?"

"Where is he?" Mel said. "I'm his brother."

One of them answered, "He is across the street in the red brick building. Noon is in there with him. As you can see, we aren't really in any shape to help him."

"You say Noon? The Texas Ranger Don Noon?" exclaimed Wadez.

"Yes, the same, but he is a deputy US marshal now," the crippled one said. "What can we do for you?"

Wadez said, "You can tell the marshal that a man that you didn't know who he was came along and told you that Noon needed to turn his prisoners loose. Otherwise, the Yost girl and her Apache friend will die."

The crippled man came back with "I thought that Tommy Quinn was on a trail drive to Montana. I understand that his brother showed up here from Arizona a few days ago."

Wadez came back with "I guess her and that boy was telling the truth. Tell Noon not to follow those men, or the two youngsters will die."

Mel Wadez walked back around the corner and up the ally. When he was out of town, he got into a willow thicket and sat to watch the goings-on.

An hour later, the crippled man yelled at Noon as he came out of his office. When Noon got over to him, he asked, "What can I do for you?"

"You can turn your prisoners loose and not follow them when they leave town."

The deputy said, "And why would I do a dumb thing like that for you?"

"A man stopped by this morning and told me that if you didn't do just that, that Sally Yost and the young man with her would die. I don't know who he was or where he went. That was his whole message. I guess that it is up to you what you want to do. I had never seen this man before."

Noon said, "You had better be telling me the truth. You had also better not of had anything to do with this." He turned and went to get his horse. He stopped by the café and picked up a couple of sandwiches to take along. He headed out of town to the Yost ranch.

It was late in the day when he rode up to the house. Bob saw him ride up and stepped out on the porch. "What can I do for you today, Marshal?"

Noon came back with "You can tell me where Sally and Billy are."

Bob questioned, "What have they done to get you to ride clear out here from town so late in the day?"

"I was told that I was to turn Con Wadez and his bunch loose from jail, or Sally and Billy would be killed. I was also told not to follow them when they left town."

Bob told Noon to come into the house. "You might as well sit and have a bite. We were just sitting down to eat supper. The kids should have been here, but sometimes, they run late. They should be here by dark."

As Don Noon sat and watched Bob and his family, he wondered what he should do.

Bob looked at him and asked, "You are wondering if you should turn that bunch loose, aren't you?"

Don said, "If someone has them, I don't want to be responsible for getting them both killed. On the other hand, I don't just want to turn killers loose."

Mrs. Yost said, "You just answered your own question. If they don't come home, then they have them. They are killers and will kill them if they have not already done so. Is it worth taking a chance on not turning them loose?"

After waiting until ten o'clock, he rode back into town and walked into the jail. He opened the door, and the men walked out, wondering why he was turning them loose.

Noon said, "I am turning you loose without your guns. Your horses are tied outside. If I find out you hurt those kids, this world isn't big enough to hide in."

Con smiled and said, "I'm not sure what is going on, but I hope I never see you again."

48

# CHAPTER ELEVEN

Bill Wilson sat across the fire from the cook and said, "Cookie, I'm sure glad you came along on this trip. You make the trip worth coming on."

Cookie smiled and said, "I'm glad I came along also. I'm glad you found that Tommy Quinn. I don't think I could have swum that river. He has always been there, making things work for us. We have had no problems on this whole trip because of him."

The hands around the fire nodded their heads in agreement.

Bill said, "The thing is that we never see him. He just steps in and scares me, and no one ever knows he is here."

"Maybe he no likes my cooken. He has only eaten a couple of meals with us for this whole trip. I don't know what he eats. He doesn't even carry a gun to shoot his meals. Maybe he is just waiting for us to tell him thank you."

"That would be nice, but I just thank you all for letting me come with you," he said, looking at them from the corner of the chuck wagon.

Bill choked on his coffee that was halfway down his throat. "How long have you been standing there listening to us, Tommy?"

Tommy said, "Long enough to know I appreciate you too. Cookie, I do like your cooking. I guess I just like the food I find along the trail. I never have to use a gun, so I don't use one."

Bill said, "Tommy, we are going to come to the Arkansas River in a couple of days. Are we going to have a flood when we get there like last time?"

49

Tommy said, "The rain will come a couple of days later this time. Maybe large rainstorms. We will get across the river all right. I have found a good crossing already."

"That puts my mind to rest for now," Bill said. "You had better sit down and get a plate full of Cookie's stew. He is getting to think you don't like his cooking."

As he got the plate and was eating the hot stew, he said, "I worry about the storms. The one across the river and those that follow."

Bill asked, "What about the ones that follow?"

Tommy just sat and looked up at the sky and said, "It is a feeling I have inside me. I will keep an eye on them. They will come, you know?"

Again, Bill asked, "Who?"

"Con Wadez and the others."

One of the hands looked at Tommy and said, "That is crazy. That US Deputy Don Noon put them in jail. Nobody could get away from him. You talk like he just opened the door and let them out."

"Maybe!"

Bill said, "We will just have to watch for them. I trust Tommy to know when they come and take care of it. Let's get some sleep. Tomorrow comes early."

Tommy Quinn walked out of camp and went into the dark. Everyone watched and wondered why he never slept in camp. Tommy needed to be where the sounds of the night could be heard.

Two days later, Tommy sat on his horse on a hill overlooking the Arkansas River. He waved at Bill Wilson and headed down to talk to him.

Tommy came up to Bill and said, "I will head upriver about a mile to the best crossing. It is wide, and the bottom is solid. We can get across tonight and be ready to go on tomorrow morning. Another day, the storm will hit. We will have to watch the herd."

All was going well as they moved on the next two days. The afternoon of the second day, Bill pointed at the large black clouds to the west. Tommy rode up to him and said, "Maybe you ought to push the cattle hard for a couple of hours. They would get tired for the night early."

Bill said, "You don't think that these cattle have ever been wet before in a rainstorm. They should be all right."

Tommy tried again, "There is a good grove of trees a few miles ahead for cover along a creek. Maybe we can get out of the rain. I don't like to get wet."

Bill laughed and with a smile, waved him on. The next two hours, the clouds built and were black with white clouds hanging down out of them. The wind started picking up, and cattle became nervous. They started to move faster with the wind whipping around.

Then it happened. It got darker and darker like the sun was going out of sight. A bright flash hit the ground beside the cattle—a sharp crack and a roar then another. The cattle took off in a stampede.

Tommy was out in the front and took the lead. He moved in on the head cow and turned her to the right. He was trying to turn them like he had turned the buffalo when he lived with the Apache.

Bill noticed him and headed to help him. That is when another bolt of lightning hit to their right. The cows turned suddenly to the left. Bill and several of the others were suddenly in the middle of the stampede.

Tommy saw Bill in the herd and moved back beside Bill. That is when a cow came under Bill's horse, and he went down. Tommy jumped from his horse and grabbed Bill as the horse rolled over him. Tommy grabbed his boss and pulled him over the horse and held Bill out of the stampeding cattle. The cattle piled over the horse. When several had built up, the herd started splitting and moved on around the horse and down cattle.

It took a couple of hours, and the herd were circled by the hands and settled down. Luck was with them that day. The cook wagon had been following the herd and was out of harm's way. Cookie followed along and watched for fallen critters.

Cookie came upon three of their men and their horses. The men were dead, and two horses had broken legs and one a broken neck. Cookie could see a pile of cattle ahead of him. As he drove up, Tommy stood up and flagged him down.

Cookie stood up and looked down at the dead horse. He realized it was Bill's. Tears came down Cookie's face. "Where is the boss, man?" Then he saw the feet sticking out past the rear of the horse.

Tommy said, "I need your help getting him into the wagon to take care of him."

Cookie asked, "Is him still alive?"

That is when he heard a groan, and one of the legs moved. Cookie was off the wagon and at Bill's side.

"You know, boss, you scare five-year-off-old Cookie. I think you dead. You have broken arm and leg. How you going to ramrod this outfit now?"

Bill tried to put on a smile but failed miserably. Then said, "You and Tommy will keep us going. If I had listened to Tommy a few hours ago, this wouldn't have happened."

Tommy's horse came walking up to him. Cookie looked at that and said, "Your horse not get hurt when run over in stampede."

Bill said, "His horse never got run over. Tommy jumped off him when I went down and grabbed me to put me behind my horse. That is the only thing that saved my life."

Cookie said, "Maybe him worth a lot to you, boss. Maybe you won't be able to pay what he is worth. Let's get the boss into the wagon. Boss, three of the men got caught in the stampede and killed."

Tommy said, "Cookie, up a couple of miles, there are some trees where we can camp for a day or two while we take care of this mess. There is a small town east of here. I'm going to go see if there is a doctor there. Also, if the men come back, have them dress these crippled and dead cows out, and I'll see if the town can use the meat."

Bill turned to Cookie and said, "He's already acting like a boss."

*****

Tommy rode into town. People looked at him with his muddy and torn clothes. He rode up to a man on the boardwalk and asked, "Do you have a doctor here in this town?"

The man said, "There is a Miss Perkins that has some schooling as a nurse back east."

Tommy said, "We had a man caught in a stampede, and he has a broken leg and arm. We also had several cattle with broken legs and a couple killed. I told the men to dress the cattle out. You can have them if you could use them. We also have three men that weren't so lucky. Maybe you can help us bury them. Now where is this Miss Perkins?"

"I'm right here. I will get my horse and some supplies and go with you," she said.

The town marshal stepped up and said, "Miss Perkins, what makes you think this man is telling the truth?"

She looked at Marshal Hales and said, "I'm going to help, and if any of you are man enough, you can follow and get some free beef to feed this town. The last I knew, we have not had much to eat around here lately."

# CHAPTER TWELVE

It had been a day since Sally and Billy had been tied to the tree. They were wondering if someone was going to come back and untie them. Or would Mel Wadez come back and kill them as he had threatened?

Billy said, "Even if Deputy Noon turns those men loose, that doesn't mean the men will come back. We may just die here tied to this tree, starving to death."

Sally said, "We can't die. I have to marry Tommy Quinn. I love him. He told me that he would come back to me."

Billy looked over to her and replied, "I didn't know you felt that way about my brother."

"Well, I do. I know he loves me too. I wish he was here now. He could save us," she assured him.

"What makes you think that he would want to marry you? Besides, even if Noon turns those men loose, what says they won't come back and kill us anyway?"

Sally sat and thought about that for a while then replied, "What would Tommy do if he were here and tied up? He would figure out something. He always is able to take care of any situation he is in."

Billy came back with "We have tried to get loose. What else can we do?"

Sally thought for a while. There just had to be a way. She started thinking of a way to get the ropes off. "Never, never, never give up" went through her mind. What would Tommy Quinn, the Apache, do? What would an Apache do? There just had to be a way out of this mess.

Billy said, "All I would need is one hand loose if I could get it untied."

Sally thought what would a cat do if he was in this situation. He would claw his way out. That was it. She had claws. She started scratching at the rope around her wrist. Two hours later, the rope started to come loose.

"Billy, I'm going to untie this rope. Like a cat, I'm going to claw this rope off one of my hands. This is what an Apache would do!" she screamed.

Billy asked, "Are you just going to turn Apache and then take the ropes off?"

"Yes, yes, I can," she said as she pulled her right hand loose. She reached over and finished taking the left hand loose. With that, she untied her legs. Then she untied Billy.

He came back with "An Apache like Tommy."

Sally smiled and got up and made her way toward where the horses had been taken. "We have to find where they took our horses."

He said, "Lead the away Apache scout."

An hour later, they were on their horses. She said, "We had better not follow the trail that Mel did. He may be coming back in the same direction. We need to stay out of sight and not skyline ourselves."

They rode up to the top of the ridge and looked down the trail Mel Wadez had gone toward town. There was a movement by the creek a half mile down near the bottom. Sally pointed it out. They moved back to the other side of the hill. She got off her horse and let him hold the reins.

She said, "You hold the horses here out of site. I'll go watch what is coming up the other side."

She lay there on her belly, watching from behind a bush. There were three men and horses heading toward the place where they had been tied. She watched for five minutes and then worked her way back over the hill. She grabbed the reins of her horse and swung on. She waved at Billy as she headed for home and away from the gang.

*****

Deputy Noon was at the Yost ranch talking to Bob. He had turned the gang loose as Mrs. Yost had asked. *What would be the next move?* Noon thought.

Bob said, "We need to find those kids. They may be tied up somewhere."

Mrs. Yost sat crying and said, "Or may be already dead."

Deputy Noon said, "Let's keep a positive attitude about this. They are not dead until we find them that way. And we won't find them that way. We can't take a chance on following them, at least for a while. If they are watching, they might just kill them."

Bob asked, "Where would that group go? They seem to want to follow Tommy and Bill Wilson to get even."

The deputy said, "I will just wait here for a few hours. If the kids come home, I'll be here. If they don't, I'll go looking."

Bob looked at his wife then back to Don and said, "I want to go with you. I couldn't just sit here and worry myself to death waiting for you."

The deputy asked, "Could I get you to get something to eat and drink to take along? I'm not sure how long we'll be. If we find Sally and Billy, I'm sure they will need some food and water."

Mrs. Yost got up and got some ham and some bread together. She asked, "Bob, would you get a couple of the canteens that are hanging in the barn and fill them with fresh water?"

A breeze started to blow, and storm clouds were coming up over the horizon. Bob pointed at the clouds and said, "If we are going to find them, we need to get going before that storm hits. There might not be a track left once that comes through."

"I guess we will go to the pond on the north range where we have been having cattle stuck in the mud. A rain would really help that area if it was to rain and fill the waterholes," Bob said.

They both mounted their horses and headed north.

*****

Mel Wadez rode up above where he had left Sally's and Billy's horses. He said, "I left those horses tied to those trees at the bottom of the draw. Let's go see where they have gone."

Con looked for tracks around where the horses had been tied. The grass didn't leave a clear picture of what had happened. He asked, "Where did you leave the youngsters tied? It sure would be good to have them to take along. When we get caught up with that trail herd, we would have some bargaining power."

Mel turned his horse east to where the hostages were tied. As they rode, he said, "I tied them up so they couldn't get loose. It would have taken a wildcat to get out of those knots."

Ten minutes later, they sat and looked at the ropes lying on the ground. As Con looked at the ropes, they noticed that one of them had been clawed to shreds.

Con said, "You said something about a wildcat. Maybe a hellcat would have been a better way to describe it after looking at the way that rope was shred."

Mel studied the tracks and made a decision, "Those two headed for their horses. If they were the ones that got those mounts and went home, we had better be out of this country."

Con turned his horse north toward Montana and headed off in a long trot. "If they get back and that Deputy Noon gets on our trail, we had better be several hundred miles from here."

# CHAPTER THIRTEEN

Tommy turned to Miss Perkins and said, "I am Tommy Quinn. I work for Bill Wilson, the trail boss. He is the man that has a broken leg and a broken arm."

"My name is Trinn Perkins. I have worked as a doctor's helper in Boston. I'm probably the most qualified to help. We need to go down to my cabin, and I'll get some riding clothes on and gather up a few things I might need."

Tommy waited outside on the porch while she retrieved her bag full of items. She came out and headed for the general store and café. Coming up to the door, she turned to a man in a chair on the boardwalk and asked him to go saddle her horse and bring it to the store for her.

As she walked in, she grabbed Tommy's hand and said, "Follow me. I need to buy some things in the store." When they got inside, she asked the owner if he would help pick out Tommy a new pair of pants and a shirt, along with some underclothes and socks. She then turned and walked over and picked her out a coat and hat.

Tommy said, "Why are you buying me clothes?"

She looked at him and said, "Looks like that stampede pretty well ruined those. Besides, clean ones would look better on you."

"I have never had new clothes in my life that I remember. Unless you call the buckskins, I wore from the chief's wife."

She looked curiously at him then said, "Let's go over and talk to the café owner."

The store owner handed her a flour sack with the items as they walked out. Walking into the café, she walked up to the owner and said, "There was a stampede, and some cattle were crippled, and some killed. I need to help doctor up a hurt man. Could you get your wagon and head west and follow us? You can have the beef. There will be two or three all skinned for you. I would appreciate it if you would bring these bags and the one out on the steps of my personal things and deliver them for me. The only thing I ask is that you get there tonight. Could you make Tommy and me a sandwich to eat on the way?"

The owner, Will, said, "I would be more than glad to go give you the help you need. I already have my horses hitched to my wagon out back, Miss Perkins. I will grab some help and head that way in fifteen minutes."

Will had his help and everything loaded. They met her and Tommy at the edge of town. The marshal rode up and demanded what they thought they were doing. He said, "You know that there have been Indian hunting parties spotted west of here. I should not let you go."

Trinn looked at him then said, "You are not in charge of me whether I go or not. You can't order me around. First of all, the town ends about a hundred feet behind us. Second of all, you are not my husband, and you never will be."

Trinn rode beside Tommy as they headed west. They were visiting as they rode. "Tommy, you said something about the clothes from the Indians. What did you mean?"

Tommy explained, "When I was six, I was kidnapped by the Apache. I was raised by the Apache chief for ten years. I was shot up in a settlement raid and left for dead. The Yost family took me in and saved my life. They taught me to read, and I lived with their family for another six years."

She asked, "I guess that that is why seeing Indian hunting parties doesn't bother you. How do you protect yourself? I notice that you don't carry a gun."

"I've never needed a gun to protect myself. I talk my way out or just walk through my troubles with my feet," he answered.

Five miles out of town, they all came over a hill and came face-to-face with a hunting party of four men. The helpers in the wagon reached down for their guns.

Tommy shouted, "Put those down and leave them down!" He looked over at Trinn and said, "Hold up here, and I will talk to these men. They will help us with the cattle."

He kicked his horse away from the group and rode up to the hunting party, holding his hand up in friendship. As he rode up, one of the braves held up a hand and then smiled. Tommy rode up to him and started talking to the head brave for a few minutes. The brave held out his hand and took Tommy's arm in a hold with Tommy doing the same to him.

After five minutes, three of the braves turned and headed back over the hill on the run. The brave, Three Feathers, came riding back to the wagon and Trinn.

Trinn looked at Tommy then ask, "What is going on?"

"This is my friend that I was raised with as a young man. His name is Three Feathers. He will go help us load the cattle for you. The other braves are going to get their families and come and take care of the other cattle that are hurt or dead. They need food just like the town does. Let's get going," Tommy said.

Two hours later, they rode up to where Tommy had left Bill. Bill wasn't there, nor was his saddle. His horse lay dead. There were three cows piled up. They were all dressed out.

Tommy turned to the people on the wagon and said, "Pull up here, and we will load two of the cows in your wagon."

The helpers and Tommy with Three Feathers helped load the two cows. Tommy told Three Feathers to look back to the south and some to the north and find the other cows for his family. He told him to come to the cook wagon and see if any others needed to be cut off because they were crippled.

He told Will to follow them up to the cook wagon and unload Trinn's bags. Trinn headed north beside Tommy.

She said, "I see why you are so good. You treat even the red men like your brothers. I can see that they are good men and have families that they love."

A couple of miles north, they could see the camp. They rode in to find Bill's skin white, and his leg and arm were swollen. Trinn jumped off her horse and went to work with Bill. She ordered, "You men get him on a couple of blankets."

She looked at Bill and said, "Hold on. This is going to hurt." She set the leg with a pull. Bill passed out. With cloth from the bag she had brought, she wrapped the leg and put two sticks alongside the leg.

She then splinted the arm so it couldn't move. She then covered him to keep him from going into shock. She said, "Cookie, when he wakes up, I have some pain medicine for Bill."

Tommy said to Will, "You can take the wagon back to town."

Will said, "I'm not so sure about those Indians."

Tommy looked at him and said, "As long as you keep your guns on the floor, just wave and keep moving toward town." He walked over and talked to Cookie, "How many cows did we lose?"

"Seven head with the cripples. The three by Bill's horse and three back where the lighting first hit. We have one crippled in the herd still. The three back where the lighting hit were dressed first, and we will butcher the one in the herd tomorrow or the next day for us, depending on Bill," Cookie answered. "Also, we buried the three men and picked up their saddles."

"I will ride back in the morning and tell the Indian families where they are. They will camp by the dead cattle and take care of them for their families. Tell the men that they are back there and not to get excited when they see them," Tommy said as he turned to check on Bill.

Looking at Trinn, he smiled and said, "I owe you big thanks for coming out and helping Bill. That marshal sure didn't want to let you leave town."

Trinn smiled back, saying, "I'm the one who should be giving the thanks. He thinks he owns me and runs the town with an iron hand. I have tried to leave and get away from him before. He had beaten me when no one was around. I just want you to know that I'm not going back."

"Where will you go?" he asked.

"I'm going on a trail drive to Montana, I guess. That is if you'll let me. Bill will need a nurse for a while. I was hoping he wouldn't mind if I just became part of this outfit."

Tommy studied her for a few minutes then said, "It's okay with me. I'm sure Bill will need some help. The only problem I can foresee is the cowhands."

She questioned, "You think they would object my riding along? I was raised on a ranch and knew how to ride a horse well and work cattle. I'm sure I can handle my end on this."

He answered with a smile and said, "It's not that you can't hold up and do what you need to do. You are good at doctoring, and I sure noticed you sit a horse really well. Trinn, it is that you are just so darn cute and right down beautiful. When stuck among all these men, they may just be watching you and letting the cattle all walk over a cliff."

She smiled back and said, "Does that include you, Tommy Quinn? Thank you for the compliment. I guess no one has ever told me that I was beautiful like that."

"I guess I have never told a woman it that way." He smiled back. "Let's check Bill and get some sleep. I'll sleep over on the other side of the wagon. Why don't you sleep here next to Bill so you can keep an eye on him?"

Tommy could hear Bill groaning in the middle of the night. He got up and walked over and knelt down beside him. He laid a hand on him then noticed Bill was burning up with a fever. He looked up to see Trinn watching him.

"He is burning up with a fever. Trinn, do you have anything to stop the fever?"

She looked up and replied, "I don't have. All I can really do is get some cold water and bath him to cool him off."

Tommy stood up and said, "I know what to do. I'll go get some help. I'll be back later this morning. You take care of him while I'm gone."

She watched him as he stood up and turned and walked toward his horse.

It was breaking daylight as he rode into the Indian camp. He stopped and whistled. He sat there for a few minutes. Three Feathers walked up beside him. Tommy said, "I need some help. Bill, the man that has the broken leg and broken arm, is burning up with a fever. I would hope your people might have something to give him for it."

"My woman has some roots and plants she makes into a drink. She also puts some on the skin to break the fever. I will send her with you to help."

Tommy said, "There are three more head of cattle to the south of here. That will give you four for your family. I brought you a paper to show that you own the cattle that we gave you."

Three Feathers told Tommy, "Thanks for the cows. The rest of the families will work on the cow that was left and then go after the other three." He asked, "Can we have the dead horses?"

Tommy said, "You can skin them for their hides and whatever you want. They are yours if you want them."

Within an hour, Pretty Feather was ready with a leather bag tied around her waist. She jumped up behind Tommy, and they headed north with a wave of thanks to Three Feathers.

Trinn looked up to see Tommy come riding into the cow camp with a woman's arms wrapped around him. Why did that bother her so much? There was a feeling she didn't quite understand.

As Tommy rode up, the Indian woman slid off the horse with him giving her a hand down. "Trinn, this is Pretty Feather. She is Three Feathers's wife. She has some Indian medicine to take away the fever. How is Bill doing?"

"He is still burning up. He is awake now, but his head doesn't know what is going on because of the fever."

Tommy walked over to the fire and got a cup of hot water and brought it back to Pretty Feather. She took it and opened her bag and took some ground powder and put it into the cup. She took her finger and mixed it up. She then walked over to Bill.

She told Tommy in her own language that Trinn couldn't understand for him to help Bill sit up. When he was up, she reached down and took hold of Bill's nose and shut off the air. When he opened his mouth for air, she poured the mixture down his throat.

He gagged and looked up to her and tried to say something, but it just wouldn't come out. He couldn't fight everyone off, but he tried. Trinn said to him, "Don't screw up that arm. I had enough trouble getting it fixed last night."

It finally came out when he asked, "Who are you, and who is this Indian that tried to poison me? What terrible stuff."

Pretty Feather said to Tommy in her Apache tongue, "He really like my medicine." Then she smiled.

Tommy repeated back what she had said with a smile. He laid Bill back down. He was all worn out. *What kind of humor did this Indian have, and who was she?* Bill thought.

Cookie walked around to the back side of the cook wagon so no one could see him laugh.

Tommy Quinn got on his horse and rode around the cattle as they were grazing. Lynn Bakken, the man that Bill had leading the men during the trail drive, rode up to Tommy and asked, "How's the boss doing today? Is he going to be up to moving by tomorrow?"

Tommy replied, "I'm not sure. We will see how he is doing in the morning."

Lynn said, "We have to start moving these cattle north on fresh feed. The Indians that some of the men saw are a worry to me."

Tommy replied, "The Indians are the least of our worries. The chief's wife, Pretty Feather, is in camp, doctoring Bill right now. She just gave him some medicine to take care of his high fever. I gave them four of the cattle you men dressed out. Two more went to the café back in town."

*****

Marshal Hales, the town's only law, talked to two of the men in the town that owed him some favors, "You need to ride out with me as my deputies and check on Miss Perkins. We are going to go bring her back. Quinn must have kidnapped her, or she would have come back otherwise. I was told he is in on this with a bunch of Indians."

# CHAPTER FOURTEEN

Deputy Noon and Bob Yost rode toward the waterholes that had the most trouble. Bob said, "I hope we can follow the tracks to where Sally and Billy were held at."

Noon came back with "We have to find where they were picked up and taken to. Then we can go from there. This rain may just wash away all the sign we had."

Several hours later, they rode up to a waterhole. Bob said as he rode a little closer, "There is a rope lying on the ground. They wouldn't have just left it here. This must be the starting place."

Noon rode around the area and saw a lot of horse tracks. Most were heading north. He said there are two sets of tracks going the north direction. They headed up the draw, following the half-washed out tracks. A half mile up the draw, they came to a tree with a shredded rope lying beside it.

"Two tracks came down the draw here and then headed north. That had to be Con. With only two tracks, they must not have the kids," Noon said.

Bob headed on up the draw, following the way that the tracks had come from. Fifteen minutes later, they could see where the horses had been tied.

Noon said, "Here, there are two sets of tracks heading back toward home. We must have missed them."

Bob said, "See here, Don, these two sets head off to the west up the hill. It has to be the kids. They didn't want to head straight for town and run into the men you turned loose."

After a mile, they saw where the horses had stopped near the top of a ridge. They then headed toward home. Then they headed into a hard run.

Bob said, "They are heading for home. Let's head in that direction. Maybe we can be home out of this rain by dark."

"I hope we read those tracks right. If not, I'll be looking for tracks for a week and probably won't find anything but more lost trails," Noon said.

Three hours later, they rode up to the corrals at the ranch to find two familiar horses looking over the fence at them. Bob said, "Let's get these horses in the barn and unsaddled. Then let's go find a warm house and a hot cup of coffee to warm our innards."

Sally threw her arms around her dad as he walked through the door. She then backed away and looked at Deputy Noon and said, "I think they were going to kill us. That brother of Cons rode up on us and took us and tied us up."

Noon looked at her and asked, "You said brother? Where did he come from?"

Sally nodded. "He said his name was Mel Wadez."

Billy said, "That girl, acting like an Apache, clawed her rope right off her hands like a wildcat. That is how we got loose. She asked me what would Tommy do. Then she did it."

Sally said, "We got off the trail where Mel headed into town in case he came back. We watched the three of them ride below us. Then we headed for home."

Deputy Noon looked puzzled then said, "We only saw two sets of tracks head north. I wonder where the other two went to. With the way the downpour is, there won't be a track left to follow come morning. I'm just glad you are both safe."

*****

Mel Wadez looked over his shoulder to see nothing but hills. Deputy Don Noon was not there. Mel said to his brother Con, "I am getting tired of looking over my shoulder for that Noon to show up."

Con Wadez said to him, "Maybe we need to quit doing what he expects us to do. He knows that we will probably head for Montana to go after Bill Wilson and that Apache kid, Tommy Quinn. Let's get smart and move in a different direction. We need to just head for a train or take a stage to Cheyenne to get ahead of those two and be waiting for them."

Mel countered, "Or maybe we could head straight for California or Oregon like Quinn told you to. We could change our names and get a new start."

"I swore that I would kill that Quinn if it is the last thing I do," Con said. "Nobody takes and makes a fool out of Con Wadez and gets away with it."

"Seems to me that he has already done that. We may be just bigger fools to give him another chance," Mel answered. "I wonder why Noon hasn't shown up yet."

"Maybe when the others split, he followed their tracks to who knows where. Maybe he has caught them and is on our trail by now. Let's head toward the mountains, and when we get somewhere, we can sell these horses and get on that stage for Cheyenne."

Mel argued, "I don't like it. I am wanted for kidnapping, and maybe the kids are home, and they will forget it."

Con said, "You broke me out of jail. Don't forget that."

"I did not. That Deputy Noon just turned you loose. I wasn't even there." Mel smiled.

"You have to remember that Noon won't forget you made a fool out of him. He will be on your case, and he will be on mine as well. Let's head for Cheyenne."

# CHAPTER FIFTEEN

Bill was lying in the cook wagon, not being very comfortable. Cookie looked back into the wagon and said, "You doing all right, boss? Maybe we need to get one of those half-broke horses in and ear him down for you."

"I'll just be glad when we stop for lunch. I guess that the cattle are all heading north. Have you seen Tommy this morning?" Bill asked weakly.

"Boss, he was gone before dawn this morning. He must not like my cooking very well. He never even takes lunch from me for days at a time. I don't think he has eaten more than six meals on the whole trip," Cookie replied.

At lunch, the wagon stopped, and Cookie had some biscuits and some beef roast from that last crippled cow. The hands just stopped over to get a quick lunch and were back to trailing cows.

They had been on the move for two days. It felt good to the hands. Bill was still surviving the bouncing over the brush and grass clumps.

*****

Tommy watched the three men following the herd. They were a day behind but not having to herd cattle. They would catch the herd by noon tomorrow. It was growing dark. Tommy moved in on their camp after dark.

As Tommy came in on the camp, Marshal Hales was saying, "I'm going to arrest that Indian lover, Quinn. I know he forced Miss Perkins to stay with him at the trail drive. I really don't think she was needed here. If she was, she would have been through and back to town."

The deputy said, "We will do whatever you say, Hales. We know where we stand. We owe it to you."

Hales came back with "You bet you do. I have wanted posters on both of you boys. I'm not sure what we will run into when we get into their camp. Two things for sure is that I want that girl to go back with me, and I want Quinn to go back in cuffs to town."

"Riding in on them with all those hands won't be that easy," the deputy said.

"We should be in there at about noon, and that girl will be in the wagon, and Quinn will probably be hanging all over her. I will get her. She thinks my authority stopped in town. My authority stops where I say it does."

The deputy came back on Hales comment, "You said that kid didn't even carry a gun. His mommy must not have given him one to play with growing up. How hard can it be?"

Tommy lay on the ground, listening to their boasts. A couple of hours later, he had three horses head and tailed. He headed back south toward Three Feathers camp. He could have them halfway there by morning. He then decided to turn them loose. He untied the rope and dropped them on the ground. He then took his rope and whipped them toward town.

Sitting on his horse on a ridge out of sight, he watched the three head for town. He could hear the marshal shouting at the two, "Couldn't you even tie the horses up? I ought to make you walk all the way back to town."

He said, "I did see moccasin tracks by where we had them tied. Maybe those hunting parties stole them. Anyways, we have to walk too."

That evening, Hales looked up and saw the horses eating in some grass by a creek. They worked in on them and caught them. They started back to their saddles and bedrolls.

He said, "You know I've been thinking, somebody turned these horses loose. They didn't all just untie themselves. I'll bet that that Apache kid did this."

*****

Tommy rode up beside Trinn. "You ride pretty well. I guess that Bill hired you on because he was short of a few hands."

She jumped at the voice then said with a smile, "Do you always scare people like that? I haven't seen much of you for a couple of days. Where have you been?"

"Enjoying watching your old friend who was coming to visit you," he said.

"And who might that be?"

He answered, "Marshal Hales from town with two of his outlaw deputies. I laid and listened to them last night. The two he has with him have wanted posters on them. He is using that over their heads to help him. He is coming to arrest me and force you back to town. He says I am forcing you to stay here with me."

Trinn laughed. "You are forcing me to stay here? That is what good friendships do. I don't want to leave you."

"How's Bill doing today? I haven't had a chance to stop and see him. I did take three horses for some exercise last night. I turned them loose and headed them back toward town. They didn't seem in a hurry to go. They will probably stop and eat. I think that they will be here about dark tonight."

She asked, "What are you going to do? I won't go back."

"Like he said, I won't let you. I'm going to take you up ahead on a ridge by a stream, and we will eat supper. You will need to stay there. When I set the three packing, I'll be up to stay the night with you, if you want?"

"I would like that," she said. "You don't think the trail hands will talk and get jealous, do you? They seem to have a hard time keeping their eyes off me."

"So does Bill. He likes you a lot, you know. I even think he would like to get to know you a lot better," Tommy said with a smile.

"Let's split up and keep these cattle moving toward Montana," she interrupted. As she pushed the cattle the next few hours, her thoughts were on what Tommy Quinn had just said to her.

Didn't he like her? For sure, he had said she was beautiful. Nobody had ever made the feelings bubble up all over inside her like Tommy had. Would she be happy with him? Why had he suggested that Bill liked her? Was he trying to get rid of her?

Before she knew it, she was on her way with him. They rode north a few miles and found the place he was talking about. As they rode up to the trees, a turkey flew up in front of them. He held up his hand to have her stay. A few more feet and she saw his arm come from behind his head. The turkey came fluttering out of the tree.

Her horse spooked some. He rode up and picked up the bird. In two minutes, he had the turkey dressed and ready to cook. He rode down by the creek and cut a heavy green willow. With salt and pepper on the bird, he had the fire going and the bird cooking within twenty minutes.

He took his bedroll off his saddle and told her that would give her a place to keep warm tonight. In another hour, they were eating a good meal.

"I can understand why you have only eaten a few meals at the cook wagon. I couldn't believe how you got that bird. I saw you reach up by your ear, and the bird came fluttering down to the ground. I never saw the knife go through the air. You are such a good cook, Tommy Quinn," she said with a smile.

"I had better get back to the cook wagon. My job is to protect Bill and the men," he said.

She stood up and walked over to him. She wrapped her arms around his neck and gave him a big kiss on the lips. She then stood back and said, "You come back to me, Tommy Quinn."

*****

Bill was propped up against the tongue of the wagon when the strangers rode in. They demanded that Bill turn Miss Perkins and Tommy Quinn over to him.

71

Tommy walked past between Cookie and Bill up to within four feet of the three men.

Tommy said, "Looks like you rode a long way to get Miss Perkins, Marshal. She left here for Wyoming. She said you had beat her and held her against her will back in that town you own. What is the charge you have on me about holding her against her will? You have no business here, so head back for the town while you can. You can go riding on those horses or tied across them. You have one minute to decide."

The marshal said, "You are under arrest for interfering with the law. I still think you are holding her against her will."

"Do you think that the three of you are men enough to take me in? When I put you across your horses, I will turn them loose, and you had better hope they go back to town and not stop to eat," Tommy said.

The marshal reached for his gun. Tommy jumped and spun and kicked him behind the ear. The other foot caught the deputy in the jaw, and he went flying back. The other deputy had his gun coming up when it went flying out of his hand with a foot catching him in the throat. As he went down, Tommy spun and kicked him alongside the head.

The men sat there with their plates in their hands, and their mouths were hanging open. They looked at each other as if they couldn't believe what they had just witnessed.

Tommy walked over and brought the horses over and tied one to the wagon wheel. He tied the others head and tail together to the first. In ten minutes, he had the men tied across their saddles without their guns.

Bill sat there and watched Tommy grab each of the men and toss them across their saddles like they were the weight of a saddle blanket. He had never seen anyone handle a body like that. He went over to his horse and grabbed the first horse and headed south.

He turned back and said, "I'll be back in a couple of hours. I guess these men had better leave the country, or I'll stake them over an anthill the next time."

Two hours later, he rode back into the cow camp. The camp became quiet when he rode in. Bill said, "That was quite a show you put on. I can see why you said you would protect us. I guess I owe you an apology for not listening to you before the storm."

"You will believe me next time. I knew these men were coming yesterday. I took Trinn up the trail, and we had turkey dinner together. Cookie, she said she liked my cooking better than yours. Probably only because it was roasted turkey."

Cookie said, "Is there anything you can't do? I never saw anyone take down three men so fast and without a gun. Then you just tossed them over their horses with no effort. I would say we are in pretty good hands."

"I'll bring Trinn back in the morning in time to help you cowboys move those cattle. I have to check on the three and make sure they head back to town."

Bill looked at Cookie and shook his head. "Why were we so lucky to have such a man show up to help us? I wouldn't have known what to do with that town marshal. If I was him, I'd head for parts unknown. Cookie, we still like your cooking."

"How did he get a turkey without a gun?" asked Cookie.

Tommy walked into the light of a fire with a girl wrapped in his bedroll. He knelt down beside her and smiled, "I thought that you would be asleep by now."

She reached up and pulled him down beside her as she pulled the blanket back. She said, "Thanks for coming back. I waited up for you to come back. I missed you, Tommy Quinn." She then put her arms around him and gave him another kiss.

They lay there in each other's arms and went to sleep.

# CHAPTER SIXTEEN

T race Carter was a large cattleman in the Miles City area. He had over another one thousand head coming from Texas. They would be here by October. His friend, Bill Wilson, had gotten the herd together and should be halfway here by now.

Trace was headed down into Wyoming Territory to look for land to expand his empire. He had over eight thousand head and wanted more. The trouble was, there hadn't been any rain since the twelfth of April. The country was turning brown, and the grass was only one inch high on the new growth this season.

He had ridden a stage to the area around Buffalo, Wyoming. The Wyoming Stockgrowers Association had the land tied up. Or at least they had what cattle that could be grazed in the area without a range war. He got into the Casper area when he heard of the Big Horn Basin.

He decided to check it out on the way home. There was a somewhat wagon trail road up over the Big Horn Mountains. In Lander, he talked to Sim Simons, and he told Trace he would be interested in buying five hundred head of the cows.

"Let's go out to my ranch, and you can stay the night. We can work out the details of the transaction and how we will get them here."

Trace liked the ranch area and the grass in the valley along the small river to the south of Lander. Trace asked, "What is the chance that a man could buy some of the grass in this area?"

Sim said, "I have most of the grass in the area. There is some other grass in this area, but I have all the water tied up along the river from Lander to the mountains. I have the grass tied up on each side of the river that the government isn't giving to the Indian tribes."

About dusk, they rode the buggy into the ranch barnyard. Pulling up to the large log house, he waved at his wife and told her, "We have some company for supper."

Walking into a large front room, Trace noticed a painting on the wall beside the fireplace. "Who painted the picture of that mountain? It looks so real. It looks just like the mountain behind your house to the west of here."

Sim's daughter walked up to him and said, "I'm Sim's daughter, Ruth. I painted the picture a couple of years ago when I got back from school in Boston."

Sim said to Trace, "I am willing to buy five hundred head of the cattle from you to put on this land, and I have heard that there is a man over in the Big Horn Basin that would take that many cows. He is wanting to get more to put with the five hundred he brought from Texas a few years ago."

"I believe the man lives south of Warmwater that is on the Stinking Water River next to the mountains on the west side of the Basin. That would get you out of a bind," Simons said. "I believe his name is Snyder."

Trace said, "I'll take a chance and go see him. I'll let you buy these cows for twenty dollars a head. You will have to pay Bill Wilson for trailing them here from Texas. I'm not sure what he will ask for trailing them. I know him, and he will be fair. Have the crew cut off the cattle when he gets here. Bill Wilson can trail the balance to Warmwater. I hope Snyder wants them."

Simons asked, "Trace, how will Bill Wilson know to come to Lander with the cattle?"

"I will get hold of Bill when he gets to Cheyenne. I'm sure the sheriff can get hold of him when he comes past that area. I'll head to Warmwater in the morning after we go to the bank and get this settled. I'll have your banker make out a draft for my cattle when they are delivered. He can have it transferred to my bank in Miles City," Trace said.

Sim's wife and daughter rode into Lander with the two men the following morning. Trace told the daughter, "If you ever get up to Miles City, I'll pay you to paint a picture of my ranch. I would love to have you come and visit someday. Let me know when you could come, and I'll pay your way."

They took care of the business in the bank while the women did their shopping.

Sim said, "The telegraph office is across the street. You can send that wire to Cheyenne. If you're not sure where the cattle are, you want to make sure the word gets to Wilson before he gets to Cheyenne."

With that taken care of, Trace was able to arrange a ride on the stage to Warmwater for the next morning. "I will stay in town tonight so I can catch that stage early in the morning. I'm buying lunch if you are all hungry."

With that, Trace took hold of Sim's daughter's arm and escorted them up the boardwalk to the café.

*****

The young messenger from the telegraph office came running into the sheriff's office. "Sheriff Wynn Howard, you have a telegraph wire from Lander."

He opened the envelope and read.

Sheriff of Cheyenne,

This is Trace Carter from Miles City, Montana Territory. There will be a herd of cattle from Texas by the Cheyenne area within the next month. Bill Wilson will be the trail boss. Please instruct him to take the cattle to Lander, Wyoming Territory. Sim Simons has bought five hundred head of the cattle. Go to the bank with him, and they are to send a bank draft to my bank in Miles City. The arrangements have already been made. Will leave

further instructions. Probably trail the rest over
the mountain to Snyder's ranch near Warmwater
in Big Horn Basin.

Trace Carter

Sheriff Howard studied the wire for a while. If this herd was
coming, it would be the first of the season to come from Texas. He
walked over to the Silver Dollar saloon and asked the bartender if he
had heard anything of a herd coming in from Texas.

"I had a couple of men in here yesterday asking the same question. I'm not sure what they wanted with the herd. They were both
rough-looking characters. They might be someone to keep an eye
on."

Sheriff Howard asked, "Has anyone else said anything about a
herd coming in? Do you know where those two have gone?"

The bartender looked at him and said, "No, but if I hear anything of a herd, I'll let you know. As to the whereabouts of the two,
I'll let you know if I see them. You might check at the livery stable or
in the other saloons in town."

Walking down to the livery stable, he watched the people coming and going down both sides of the street. Walking through the
large door, he saw Brian setting some shoes on a horse. He watched
until he let the foot down.

Sheriff Howard asked, "Brian, have you got a couple of horses
here that have shown up in the last few days? I'm looking for a couple
of rough-looking fellas."

He answered, "I haven't seen any new horses lately, but two
men came in wanting to buy a couple of horses. They asked about a
trail drive coming through and wanted to get a job trailing the cattle
to Montana. Matter of fact, they bought two horses from me. This
is one of them. They wanted them shod and ready to go in the next
few days."

Howard asked, "Do you have any idea where I might find them?
I need to find out more about those cattle."

"I'll let you know if I see them, Sheriff."

# CHAPTER SEVENTEEN

US Marshal Don Noon put out wanted posters on the men that he let out of jail. Mostly, he was interested in two of them that had to do with Sally Yost and Billy Quinn's abduction—Con Wadez and Mel Wadez.

He should have never let Con Wadez out of his jail. Because of the pleading of Mrs. Yost for her daughter's life and Billy Quinn's, it seemed the only thing to do at the time. He would do it again if he had to. He had no daughter or wife for that matter, but he knew that life was precious. He had taken a lot of lives over the years as a Texas Ranger and then again as a US deputy marshal.

It had been a week since that day when Sally and Billy had come back after her clawing her way out of the ropes. She had to be a real wildcat to shred the ropes he saw on the ground that day.

Someday, he would have a wife and maybe a daughter. He hoped he would have a daughter as vibrant as Sally was and as beautiful as Alice Snyder.

Shaking his head, he thought, *Where did that come from?*

He knew! She was that girl he used to ride the hills with when they were kids. They would check the cows and race home some days. He even let her take the lead when trailing cows, just so he could be behind her and keep his eyes on her. She was that girl who gave him that big hug and a wonderful, never to forget, kiss while she held him in her arms before they went to Wyoming.

What he would give to see her again. She might be married and couldn't even remember him. A tear came rolling down his cheek as he remembered that day, that beautiful redheaded blue-eyed girl made him fall in love with her.

That is why he turned those men loose—for the love of a mother, for the love of a wonderful daughter who was a girl.

*****

Bob Yost needed to have the ponds checked, and the cattle rode through. He was having a hard time letting his daughter ride out again. Were those men really gone? Had they really left the country for good? Could he take the chance of letting her ride so far from home? The thoughts of those days, not so long ago, lingered deep in his mind. He had almost lost his precious daughter.

Bob looked up to see a rider coming up the road. As he got closer, he noticed Don Noon. What had gone wrong this time? Why was the marshal here? All he had this morning were questions going through his mind.

Raising a hand, Noon said, "How're things going around here today? I just got to thinking about that family of yours and couldn't get them out of my mind. So I just took a ride out to check on all of you."

Bob smiled and took his hand. "Let's put that horse of yours in the barn on a can of oats. Then we will go join that wonderful family for some biscuits and a slice of ham. Maybe even a cup of Mom's hot coffee. Not to mention the sausage gravy to go over those biscuits."

As they finished breakfast, Bob said, "I have been thinking that the cattle needed to be checked on. I just can't convince my mind to turn loose and let the kids go check the cattle again."

"Why don't you let me ride along with the two of them, and we can get a better feeling about it? If the chores are done, we will take off so we can be home by dark," Don offered.

Bob looked at Sally and said, "You two go get your horses saddled. And, Don, thank you for the offer. You going along makes me feel better about things."

As they rode along, checking the cattle, Sally said, "This is the waterhole where the man came upon us while we were pulling the cow out of the mud."

"Yes, this is where your dad and I picked up your rope on the ground. That is why we knew where to start looking for you. The waterhole is almost full now after the rains this past week."

"Let's head on east of here toward that waterhole in the far corner of our pasture. It should be full also. Billy, you have never been down there with me before," she commented.

Billy smiled at her and said, "Someday, I hope to get to ride all your range with you and get to know it. I enjoy us riding together."

Deputy Noon thought, *He probably would like to get to know this girl better than the range.* He had noticed how Billy had a hard time keeping his eyes off of her. He had watched her a lot more than the range and the cattle on it.

As they came down to the waterhole that she led them to, he noticed there were no cattle around it. Noon said, "I sure don't see any cattle around here. I see tracks that are fresh, so where are the cows?"

She kept riding, keeping her eyes studying the ground. Then she noticed it and said, "Here are two fresh horse tracks pushing a herd of cattle and going south."

Noon rode over to study the tracks and followed them for about a quarter mile. He then said, "These tracks can't be over a few hours old. I had better follow them. It looks like someone is rustling them. Maybe the two of you had better not go with me. There may be some shooting, who knows."

She looked at him and said, "These are our cattle, and I need to help get them back. We will stay back when we catch up with the rustlers. When you arrest them, we can trail the cattle back to the waterhole."

"That will work, Sally. You sure seem to know what you are doing. With this going on, I'm glad I came with the two of you today. With the number of tracks, it's pretty clear to follow. Let's kick hind end."

Only a mile later as they came over the hill, they almost rode right into the middle of the rustlers. They hadn't seen any dust because of the recent rains.

Sally and Billy pulled up while the deputy rode up behind the men following the cattle.

He rode up and asked, "Where are we going with the cattle?"

The men jerked their heads around, and at the same time, they were pulling their guns.

Noon pulled his and shot the one with the crippled leg in the head. The other jerked as he saw his partner fly from his horse and shot past Noon's ear. Noon didn't miss. It was placed in the man's left shirt pocket. He sat there for several seconds after dropping his gun then rolled off the right side of his horse.

The cattle took off with the noise at their back side. Sally and Billy came running past the two dead men and followed Noon to get around the cattle. Within a half mile, they had them under control heading back to the pond and the range they had come from.

The deputy rounded up the two horses and went to pick up the bodies.

Sally rode over to Don and asked if she could help him load the bodies.

He said, "I guess you could hold the horses while Billy and I load them and tie them down."

Billy said, "I guess...guess so." He was a little nervous about getting his hands on the dead, bloody bodies.

Sally said to Billy, "You hold the horses, and I'll help load the bodies."

When they were loaded, Deputy Noon said, "Thanks for the help. These were two of the men that I turned loose from my jail a week ago. I guess no one will have to go looking for them now."

Don again thought, *What a spitfire of a lady.*

*****

Back at the ranch, Bob saw the three riding in and leading two horses with the bodies tied over their mounts.

"I guess I was right in not sending those two out alone." Bob then asked, "Are these two of the men you turned loose last week?"

Noon nodded his head and said, "I'm just glad you didn't send those young ones to check the cattle. Otherwise, it would have been the two of them across their horses."

Mrs. Yost came out on the porch and looked at the scene. "When is this all going to end? I have supper ready if you want to eat a bite. Are you going to stay here, Don, or are you going back to town tonight?"

"I'll grab a quick bite and then head for town. I don't want to have to load these two up again." Don tied the three horses to the corral fence and headed for the house.

"Thank you for the meal," Don said. "I'll head into town and get this mess taken care of."

# CHAPTER EIGHTEEN

"Miss Perkins, I sure want to thank you for what you did for me," Bill said. "I probably would have died if you hadn't been such a good nurse."

"I am the one to thank you for sending Tommy into town and getting me. I tried to get out of that town for months. That no-account town marshal caught me several times trying to leave. He beat me each time he caught up with me. Tommy being there made the difference."

Bill questioned, "What kind of person is he? I didn't send Tommy into town. I didn't even know that town was there. Tommy seems to know what is going on in front of us, as well as behind us at all times. You know, Miss Perkins, you are sure a beautiful young lady."

She blushed at that and said, "Tommy has told me that also. I sure like him. I hope that he likes me as much as I like him."

Bill said, "Why do you say that? I think he likes you a lot. Maybe even more than that."

As she thought about what Tommy had said to her, she said, "When I told him that I liked him, he told me that you liked me a lot. Kind of like you had your eye on me. Kind of like I should be your girl."

It was Bill's turn to blush. "I guess that would be very nice."

She said, "The trouble is, I only really have feelings for one man. That is Tommy Quinn. I want to marry him someday."

As Bill looked at her, he said, "I guess that leaves me out of the running. I have never seen such a man that knew what was going on around him as Tommy Quinn."

She said, "Except what is going on in my heart and mind for him. The night that town marshal came for me, he took me away so I didn't have to face the man. He killed a turkey with his knife at over thirty feet away. We ate the turkey that night, and I ate some of it for breakfast."

Bill said, "When he came back that night, he said you liked his cooking better than Cookie's cooking. I think that made Cookie a little jealous. He said it was probably only because it was a turkey."

She said, "Right on all accounts. The thing is I stayed up till he got back that night. I was lying on the ground under the bedroll that he had left with me. When he came over and knelt down to talk to me, I pulled him down under the blankets, and he lay there and slept up beside me all night."

Bill answered, "It looks like he didn't try to get away from you. You know, if when I have a son, I will hope he would be just like him."

"Thank you, Bill, and thanks for letting me stay with the trail drive. I'm glad I was able to fix you up. I sure enjoy moving the cows. I was raised on a ranch in Wyoming."

Bill said, "I thought you were from Boston. I guess I should have known better after watching you ride and the way you knew cattle."

She smiled and said, "I've noticed that you aren't the only one that watches me ride. My dad sent me to Boston to make a *lady* out of me. He still thinks I'm in Boston. I just couldn't stay and be in the city. I was working my way home when Marshal Hales saw me and said he would help me. Thinking he was a marshal, I figured he must be a good person. Boy, was I wrong?"

"I guess we can't make all the right decisions. Tommy told me to push the cattle hard for a couple of hours before that storm hit. I chose not to, and look what happened to me. All he said to me was that something like I'd listen next time."

"You know, Tommy is not always right. He was pushing me toward you. I like you Bill, but I guess it is him I'm in love with."

"When we get to Cheyenne, maybe he'll slow down enough for you to catch him and marry him. Do you really want your last name to be Quinn?"

She replied, "With all my heart. I just wonder if I show up at the ranch with an Indian if dad will disown me. What he really wanted was a lady. What he will get is a Trinn Quinn."

Bill said, "Trinn Quinn, that sounds pretty good to me. Doctor, do you think I can walk on this leg yet?"

"It sounds good to me," she said. "At least the name. I think you had better stay off that leg until we get to Cheyenne. We can have a real doctor check it out."

"That long?" he said.

"I guess that I had better quit dreaming and get after him. I'm not sure where he is," she said.

"I can tell you one thing I've found out about him. That is, he always knows what is going on up the trail and behind you. He always seems to walk up behind me when I least suspect it. It always scares me. I think he enjoys it," Bill commented.

"Do you think he has been listening to us? I would be embarrassed," she said.

"How do you think I get to know what is going on? How could I find out what I'm supposed to do?" Tommy asked.

Both her and Bill said at once, "Tommy Quinn, how dare you sneak up on us like that?"

Tommy smiled and said, "I guess I'm going to get married in Cheyenne. Is that why you bought me those clothes?"

Bill asked, "What clothes?"

"The ones I bought for him to change into because he was so dirty from being in the stampede. You know, when he jumped off his horse and pulled you over behind your horse to save your life. He was knocked down in the mud. He didn't take them when I bought them. I guess he found a creek since then," she said.

Bill looked at him and said, "I don't remember you doing that for me. I guess that I owe you another time for saving my life. I guess I was a little out of it."

Trinn said, "I still have the clothes for you. I think they would look very good on you at our wedding."

"Who said I was going to marry you?"

"I did. You just got to Tommy Quinn. I love you so much. I need you in my life. Do you like me?"

"Yes, I do like you," he said. "But I like Sally too."

She stopped breathing for a moment then said, "Who is Sally? I've never heard of her." She looked at Bill.

Bill answered, raising his shoulders, "I don't know any Sally."

Tommy said, "She is the girl that doctored me up after I was all shot up and left for dead. She wanted me to come back to her when we got these cattle to Montana. I like her too."

"Do you like her?" Trinn asked.

"Yes, I like her, and I like you," Tommy answered.

"Do you love her?" Trinn asked.

"I like her, but I told her I would be back by next spring," he said.

Trinn was getting frustrated when she asked, "Tommy Quinn, do you love me?"

Tommy looked over at Bill.

Bill said as he shrugged his shoulders, "I'm staying out of this. Whatever I say would be wrong. If I were your father, I would not know what to say. I don't know Sally. Your heart has to say what it will. I guess I would give it a few days and think it out in my mind."

Tommy said to Bill, "I've got to go check the three men that have been following us for a few days. I'm not sure who they are, but they need to be checked on."

Tommy got on his horse and rode south.

Trinn started to cry. "I guess I shouldn't have got so close to him. He probably doesn't really love me. He didn't answer my question."

Bill smiled and said, "Trinn, he probably doesn't really know the answer. I think the advice I gave him would be good for you as well. A few days, beautiful girl. I know the answer, but he has to find it within his heart. Be patient. You will like the answer."

She looked at Bill and reached over and gave him a hug. "Thank you. You sound like a father."

# CHAPTER NINETEEN

The sun was setting as the three men came down to the creek. It was a warm evening with the crickets making a lot of noise.

The town marshal was sitting down on the log. His head was beginning to hear the complaints of his two deputies.

The one with the loudest voice was saying, "You know the last time we tried this, we were sent home across our horses. We also had our horses turned loose."

Hales came back with "Randy, you said we didn't need to set a guard last time. Maybe you wouldn't mind having the first watch and your partner the second. Move the horses up the creek so I don't have to listen to them while I sleep."

"Which one do you take?" Randy asked.

"I'll take a good night's sleep. I'll get breakfast ready when the sun comes up. You got any objections?"

"You always get the best," Randy said.

Hales shouted back, "Then I'll take the first watch, and you fix breakfast! I'll move up the creek a few hundred yards. I don't want burnt ham if you're doing the cooking."

"Sounds fine to me," Randy said.

Listening in the bushes, Tommy set forth his plan. He always had a plan. His mind was always clear on things, except for that girl who wanted to marry him. Then he thought, *Quinn, get your head on straight. Forget about her for now. Put your mind on what you are doing.*

It had been dark for several hours. The two at the camp were asleep. Hales was watching the horses with his back to the tree. He was sitting there with one eye closed. His head was nodding every once in a while.

Tommy came up to the back side of the tree. He peeked around the tree. Hales's head bobbed again. Tommy's fist hit him like a club alongside the head. He was out.

Bound and gagged, Hales was sound asleep with his back against the tree. He would stay that way for a while.

Now it was Tommy's turn to watch the horses. He could watch them and probably even be able to catch that man that unties horses in the middle of the night. Somebody had to be on watch tonight.

Three hours later, the one called Randy came walking up to the tree. He stepped up by Hales and gave his foot a kick. "You talk about watching the horses," Randy said. "You had better get up off your lazy hind end and watch for Quinn."

"He's watching," Tommy said, standing beside him.

Randy jumped just in time to see the foot hit him alongside his head. He would join the marshal asleep all bound and gagged beside the tree.

He was walking silently with his moccasins on into the camp. There was only one more to take care of. Lying there, he had his face turned away from Tommy.

"Hales, is everything all right?"

Tommy said in his Apache voice, "All right."

The deputy came awake as he spun over just in time to catch a foot in his face. Tommy tied the man up but didn't have to gag him.

He looked through the food in a bag. He found a can of peaches that he opened with his knife. He ate them. They were so good. He opened another and ate it. He sat and closed his eyes for a couple of hours.

With daylight came a beautiful orange and red sky. There was just enough breeze to feel refreshing.

An hour later, the men were tied across their saddles and heading for the chuck wagon. It had started a wonderful day. Only seeing the look in Trinn's eyes when she saw Hales across the saddle would make it better.

The cattle were heading north with Trinn near the lead. Tommy rode up to the chuck wagon and said, "Cookie, I found something back along the trail. They wanted to go for a ride with me. I just couldn't refuse their offer."

Bill was sitting in the seat beside Cookie. He jumped at the sound of the voice. "Dang you, Quinn. Do you always have to scare me?"

"Maybe you need to be more aware of what's going on around you, boss. Thought these friends of Trinn's would enjoy riding with me to Cheyenne. She might even enjoy seeing them. They just seem to keep hanging around here."

Cookie said, "The way their heads are hanging down there, I guess hanging around is about right."

"I'm going to take them into the sheriff in Cheyenne. I hear there is a bounty on each of them. Maybe I can make some money on this here cattle drive yet. I want to see Trinn's eyes when she sees these men. Maybe she would like to turn them over to the law herself."

"She just might at that. We are only a day out of Cheyenne. Go ask her," Bill said. "You know you get her into Cheyenne, she might want to just marry you."

Tommy smiled and turned to ride off but not before Bill saw that smile on Tommy's face.

"Tommy!" Bill yelled. "Why don't you take that bag of Trinn's along? She might want them to clean up when she gets there. I'll get it for you."

Bill climbed into the back of the wagon and quickly went through Trinn's things. He got the new clothes for Tommy and put them at the bottom of the bag. Next was her dress then some clean riding clothes, along with her hairbrush. He handed it out to Tommy as he walked up to the wagon.

Bill said, "I think this is what she would want. Here is twenty dollars to help take care of her while you two are in Cheyenne."

"Thanks, Bill. I guess I wouldn't have thought of the money. I've never had any. Maybe I'll give it to Trinn to handle. She knows more about that sort of thing."

Bill smiled then said, "Go ask that girl to ride to Cheyenne with you. I'm sure she will want to go with you."

He rode up on Trinn, and she turned to look at the horses following him. Then she noticed the men across their saddles. She smiled at him and said, "This must be my birthday. Is this why you brought them to me all tied up in ribbons?"

"I'm taking them into the sheriff in Cheyenne. I remember them saying something about a wanted poster on them. I guess we will go find out," he said.

"We!" she said.

"I would like you to ride in and turn them over to the sheriff. You might just enjoy that. Bill sent a bag, along with a few of your personal items in it." He stepped down from his horse and got the bag. "You might want to check what he sent. We might have to go back and get something he forgot."

She looked through the bag and smiled when she saw the clothes that she had bought for him—the clothes for him to wear at their wedding!

"This will do just fine," she said.

"He also gave me twenty dollars for us while in Cheyenne if we need it. I told him I'd give it to you to take care of. I've never had a use for money where I have lived."

She said, "I guess that Apaches don't have much use for money." She took the money and reached up and surrounded his neck with her arms and their lips met. She didn't turn loose for more than a minute. When she stepped back, she said, "I hope you will want to marry me. I wouldn't want to go on living without you in my life, Tommy Quinn."

He took her in his arms and gave her another one of those kisses she desired.

By this time, the chuck wagon was closing in on the two of them. Bill looked over at Cookie then gave him a slap on the back and said, "I think that that boy just got his head on straight."

"Maybe when we get to Cheyenne, we can attend a wedding." Bill laughed.

That night, Trinn and Tommy rode into Cheyenne to the sheriff's office. Trinn introduced themselves to the sheriff.

"I'm Sheriff Lynn Howard. What can I do for the two of you?"

Trinn said, "We have three men that would like to get off their horses. They keep wanting to hang around me. I believe they all have wanted posters on them. If you don't have them, I'm sure you can get ahold of the posters. I want to turn them in for the reward. I would like to press charges against the one that will claim to be Marshal Hales. He has beaten me several times. He is no marshal, and these that claim to be his deputies are not deputies."

As they walked out of the office, he noticed the men hanging over their saddles. "What kind of a deal is this? How long have they been tied across their saddles like this?"

"I put them there this morning, sir. They were told when I sent them back to their town a while back that I would treat them like an Apache would if I ever saw them again. And if they ever bothered Miss Perkins again, I thought about tying them across an anthill and cutting their tongues out."

Sheriff Howard said, "What kind of an Apache are you anyway?"

Trinn said, "He is an Apache's son. Raised as an Apache chief's son for ten years. I think he could have gotten it done."

"Let's get these men off these horses and into my jail. I think that they would prefer my jail to this."

"We will be back in the morning to press the charges and see about the reward," Trinn said.

Several people had been watching as the men were taken into the jail. There were comments made about the Apache.

They left the three men and their horses to Sheriff Howard's care. They took their horses to the livery stable and got them taken care of.

They went to the Stockman's Café and got a meal. She ordered them each a roast dinner with potatoes and gravy.

The waitress looked at the two of them and said, "You look like some trail crew that haven't had a bath in several weeks. I'm sorry, I shouldn't have said that."

Trinn said, "We are. We have been with a trail herd from Texas. I just turned over three men to Sheriff Howard that needed to be locked up. I'm sure if I was back in Boston at that lady's school again, they would have said worse than that. When we get our supper, we plan on getting a room and cleaning up."

The waitress blushed and said, "Sorry, I will get you some food. I'll bet you are hungry."

The hotel was next door. Trinn asked if she could get a room with a bath. When she got the key, she walked over to Tommy and said to follow her. They went up to room 203. Tommy followed her in. She laid the bag on the bed. There was a note on the dresser that they could go downstairs to the rooms with baths for them. She picked up her bag, and they went down. There were ten small rooms with tubs and hot water that would run into them.

Tommy said to Trinn, "How do we get water in the tubs?"

Trinn ran the water into the tub for him then went to her own little room and ran her water. She sat in the water and soaked for half an hour. She went through the bag and found her clean clothes. At the bottom of the bag was Tommy's clothes. She smiled.

She got through getting dressed and walked out into the hall. She walked down to Tommy's door and knocked. "Are you there, Tommy?"

He said, "I'm here. I guess I fell asleep in that hot water. I guess I never did go to bed last night."

"I've got those clean clothes for you. Do you want to put them on?"

There was silence for a couple of minutes. Then she heard him say, "Sure, just hand them through the door, and I'll get them."

She opened the door, and he was standing there with just his pants on.

She blushed then handed him his clothes. "I'll wait out in the hall for you." She thought, *I've never seen a man with muscles like that.* She sat and waited for three minutes until he came out. She grabbed his arm, and they headed for room 203.

When in the room, she stood there, looking at him and said, "Those clothes are almost a perfect fit. The shirt is a little tight across the shoulders, but that is not the shirt's fault. You sure look good in them." She walked over to him and put her arms around his neck like she had that morning. She started to kiss him when he took her in his arms and returned the kiss. When she had no air left, she pushed him away and said, "I have to come up for air. I sure love you, Tommy Quinn. Should we try that again?" He redid the kiss as it was before.

She said, "You will have to turn and face the door until I change into my nightclothes. I guess you can sleep in your new pants for the night."

She went over to the bed and threw the covers down.

He asked, "Where should I sleep?"

"You can sleep there beside me like you did out in the hills under the trees that night when we ate that turkey."

She lay there and motioned for him to lay down beside her. When he got onto the bed, she pulled the covers up over them and put her arms around him and said, "This is the way I want to go to bed the rest of our lives. I love you, Tommy Quinn."

After two days without sleep, he was asleep before he had heard all his name. She just lay there and placed kisses on his face for an hour. Then she said before drifting off to sleep, "I love you, Tommy Quinn."

# CHAPTER TWENTY

Con Wadez and his brother sat in the saloon, listening to the gossip being said. Talk was coming from over in one corner about three men being brought into jail earlier that day. Something was said about them being brought in across their saddles—something about one of them being an Apache.

Mel Wadez said, "I guess we have found our man. Let's go to the café and get some supper before they close. We need to find him and take care of him."

Con walked into the Stockman Café and sat at a table where he could watch the front door. The waitress was sitting at a table back in the corner. She got up and walked over to the two men that looked as grubby as the man and woman that was in earlier.

"Are you with that cattle herd trailing to Montana?" she asked. "There was a young man in here earlier today that said there was a herd just south of town. We have some stew left. That is about all. The cook has gone home. The crew cleaning up and I are all that are here."

Con nodded his head and said, "That will do. No, we aren't with them, but we plan on riding out and talking to them. I hear they are short of help."

She turned toward the kitchen and retrieved two large bowls of stew. "There is salt and pepper on the table if you like. I'll go get a couple of cups of coffee."

Mel said to her, "That would be fine, and thanks for the stew. It smells good."

She went over to the table in the corner and sat back down. If no one came in, she would lock the café for the night when they left. She sat and listened to the two men discussing their plans.

She could hear the one say, "We have to stay out of sight. We need to get that Indian lover that rides with the herd."

The other asked him, "What do we do with him? We can't take care of him in town."

The other answered, "We'll take him to that abandoned barn we've been waiting in east of here. Then we'll cook him. Nobody will miss him or that old barn."

*****

The next morning, Trinn pulled Tommy's face over to hers. She placed a kiss on his lips. He opened his eyes and then smiled. He looked around to see where he was at. He was still half asleep.

He said, "I could like waking up like this every morning."

She smiled and gave him another kiss. This one lasted until she ran out of breath. "Let's go get married today so you can do just that. I love you, Tommy Quinn."

He looked into her face and said, "I love you, Trinn. I guess I have since the first time I met you. We'll go take care of that business with the sheriff first."

"You turn your back on me for a few minutes. I need to get dressed."

He turned his back and grabbed his new shirt and put it on. She put her new riding clothes on then said, "I'm ready. You really look good in those clothes. Good enough to marry." She then gave him another hug and kiss.

They walked into Sheriff Howard's office. The sheriff looked up and smiled. "You two look like you might be able to live a little today. I looked at you last night, and I wondered if you had been put through a stampede."

Trinn asked, "Did you find any posters on the men we brought in? I know they had discussed it when Tommy came to get me to take care of Bill Wilson, the trail boss."

The sheriff looked up in surprise. "You are a part of Bill Wilson's trail drive?"

Tommy answered, "Yes, I have worked for him since I joined him at Abilene, Texas. I picked up Trinn here along the way to take care of Bill. He got caught in a stampede and broke a leg and arm. She's a pretty good doctor."

Trinn cut in, "I'm really only a somewhat nurse. I worked as a doctor's assistant in Boston."

"I have a wire here from Lander, Wyoming, from a Trace Carter of Miles City, Montana. It is for Bill."

Trinn said, "Bill put Tommy in charge when he got hurt. I guess that he could read it. It won't hurt for all of us to know what is going on."

Howard handed the telegraph wire to him. It read:

Sheriff of Cheyenne,

This is Trace Carter from Miles City, Montana Territory. There will be a herd of cattle from Texas by the Cheyenne area within the next month. Bill Wilson will be the trail boss. Please instruct him to take the cattle to Lander, Wyoming Territory. Sim Simons has bought five hundred head of the cattle. Go to the bank with him, and they are to send a bank draft to my bank in Miles City. The arrangements have already been made. Will leave further instructions. Probably trail the rest over the mountain to Snyder ranch near Warmwater in Big Horn Basin.

Trace Carter

Trinn said all excited, "That will take me home. Sim Simons is a neighbor about five miles from my home."

"I think that Bill will be in town to have his leg looked at by a doctor either today or tomorrow," Tommy said.

Trinn asked, "What did you find out about the men we brought in yesterday?"

Sheriff Wynn Howard looked at them and said, "I don't know where you found these men, but they all have a line of robberies and killings that would make me not even want to take them on. They have killed a half dozen bounty hunters the past five years. The best of the best have taken them on and lost. How did you ever outdraw and outshoot these men? I don't see any evidence that anyone got shot."

Trinn said, "Tommy doesn't wear or use a gun. He is good with a knife and can fight with his feet."

Howard said, "How could a man take on three men with their reputations and come out alive? Many of the best have taken them on and lost their lives."

Tommy said, "You talk of the best. I've heard that the US Deputy Marshal Don Noon was the best. I don't think there is anyone better. I got to know him a little back in Abilene before I left."

"Talking of Noon, I hear he went into his jail in the middle of the night and turned three men loose. I understand it was because one of the convict's brothers had kidnapped a young girl and a boy that showed up from Tucson."

Tommy, shaking a little, said, "Was that girl named Sally Yost?"

Howard said, "I believe that was the name. I'm not sure of the boy's name."

"It was Billy Quinn. He is my younger brother that I haven't seen since he was four years old. He showed up looking for me after I was on the trail drive."

"Two of the men that were brothers were Con and Mel Wadez. I have wanted posters on them also," the sheriff said.

Tommy said, "I took Con to New Mexico across his saddle to turn him over to the Navajo Indians. I had a weak spot and turned him loose with the promise he would go to California. He came back, and I caught him again and turned him over to Deputy Noon. If he is loose, he will be following me."

"Don sent me a wire on him. He said he thought they would show up here in Cheyenne. A couple of grubby characters showed up a week ago. They bought two horses down at the livery stable but hadn't picked them up as of several days ago."

97

Trinn asked, "Was there a reward for the three we brought in? We need to settle this and take care of some business. Then we had better get out and warn Bill Wilson."

Sheriff Howard told them, "The total reward due you is over ten thousand dollars. The railroad has offered most of it. There are several banks that contributed and a few ranches. The State of Texas may well want to offer some also. They will probably hang because they have all been convicted of murder one time or another."

Tommy said, "That is a lot of money."

Trinn added in, "It would go a long way in getting our business started. Would you have the money sent to the Bank of Lander in my name?"

Howard said, "I thought that it was Tommy's money. I was thinking that he brought them in."

Trinn answered, "He did, but I helped. When that is done, we still have some more important business to take care of."

"And just what would that more important business that has to get done be?" Howard asked.

Both of them answered at once, "Getting married."

Sheriff Howard said, "I guess that that is important. Let's go to the bank and get this taken care of. If those two are here in Cheyenne, I had better get after my business."

When the money was transferred, they headed for the livery stable to check on the outlaw's horses. The horses were gone. The sheriff said, "Brian, I thought I ask you to let me know if they picked up those horses."

"I would have, but they said they would look me up if the law came after them. I'm sorry, but I'm just not ready to die over a couple of horses."

The sheriff just shook his head. "I understand. Now that I've been here, they might be watching, and you might still be in danger."

Tommy checked his and Trinn's horses. Seeing that they were taken care of, they headed out the door. Looking up the street, he said to Trinn, "There is Bill now with a couple of his cowboys." He let out an Apache shout that was heard halfway through Cheyenne. Bill looked up and waved.

The sheriff and the two headed down to talk to them. Bill shouted a greeting, "How are things going for you two? I came in to see that doctor like my nurse said. Cookie came in to get supplies. Where is your doctor, Sheriff?"

Trinn said, "Bill, this is Sheriff Lynn Howard. Sheriff, this is Bill Wilson, our boss."

Howard said, "Howdy, I've heard some about you. I guess we had better walk down to the doc's office and have you checked out. Miss Perkins here has a wire in her pocket that will change your life a little."

"And what would that be, Trinn? Who sent you a wire that would change my life?"

"A man named Trace Carter. He wants you to escort me home to Lander. Of course, he will want you to take the cattle along also. He has sold five hundred head of them to Sim Simons, the neighbor next to my dad's ranch. I knew you would be excited to escort me home."

The doctor took the splints off and the wrappings. He checked the leg and arm. "I'd say this girl has done a super job. Maybe she would like a job as my assistant here in Cheyenne. You can walk on this leg, but I would stay off your horse for another thirty days. Be careful with that arm."

Trinn smiled and said, "No thanks, Doctor, I have more pressing matters in my life."

"And what would that be?"

The sheriff standing beside them piped up, "Getting married in about an hour."

Bill gave her a wink and said, "Like a father's advice well taken."

Tommy looked at both of them and asked, "What advice?"

She came back with "The same advice he gave you. Sheriff, who would we talk to about getting married?"

"The Justice of the Peace would do it for you. There is a church minister, but he is out of town for a couple of days," the sheriff answered. "I'll go talk to the judge and get it arranged for the two of you."

Trinn said, "I'll go to the hotel and get my dress on. Tommy, you might want to get cleaned up a little. Bill, if you will wait in the lobby of the hotel, I'll see to Tommy getting cleaned up and send him down. I'll get my dress on and meet the two of you there with the other cowboys that came along."

Bill was a little slow on the bad leg. "Sheriff, if you will tag along with me, I might make it. There goes one of the most interesting young men I have ever met. He has saved our hide so many times coming from Texas. He only carries a knife. I don't think he even owns a gun. I've seen him take on three men, all drawing guns at the same time. He put them all flat on the ground. Then he threw them all over their horses like they were feathers. He went to an Indian hunting party and got the chief's wife to come to our camp and doctored me for a fever. He was raised as an Apache chief's son for ten years. I would take him as my son anytime. I would take that girl as my daughter as well."

Tommy came down to the lobby. Bill was sitting next to a window by a table. "You are a lucky man, Tommy Quinn. That girl will make you the best wife in the world. She told me that you tried to steer her my way. She wouldn't have any part of it. She said that you were the only one she would ever marry. She will be a great mother to help raise your children. You could even name one of your boys after me."

Trinn came down the stairs in her elegant dress that she had gotten in the lady's school in Boston. She waved at them and gave them a big, beautiful smile.

They both stood up. Tommy said, "Can I marry someone that pretty? Trinn, you are the most beautiful girl in the world."

Bill said, "If you don't, I'll take her if she will have me."

She said, "Tommy Quinn, you wouldn't want that sheriff after me for doing something bad. You try to back out, and he will be after me."

Bill cut in, "Let's go get this celebration over with. I need to get back to the herd and head them toward Lander. The two of you can stay here tonight and catch up with us tomorrow."

The marriage ceremony went like Trinn had planned. Bill stood in and gave the bride away. The judge announced them husband and wife, Trinn and Tommy Quinn. With a big hug and a kiss that she had been looking forward to, Tommy didn't disappoint her in the least.

She stepped back and said, "Just like I said my name would be Trinn Quinn."

There was a lot of laughter and a lot of love passed around. Bill looked over the gathering and handed Trinn another twenty-dollar gold piece for a wedding present. He called to his men and headed out to get the cattle drive going in the right direction.

Trinn said, "Tommy Quinn, you have made me the happiest girl in the world. I will go change into my riding clothes. You know, I could never be a lady. I can't eat and wear a dress at the same time. You go order us a chicken dinner if they have it. If not, I would settle for a big steak. You order what you want for you."

He walked into the Stockman's Café and looked around. The waitress that had served them the day before came walking up and headed him for a table in the back corner.

"I hardly recognized you. Where is that young lady you had with you last night? I guess you really know how to get all fancied up. What would you like for lunch?"

"Trinn would like chicken for dinner, and I would take the same. She is changing out of her Boston lady's school dress."

She questioned, "Where did she get a dress like that? That would be a little out of place in Cheyenne, Wyoming."

Tommy smiled and said, "That dress came with that girl from Boston, and she looked absolutely beautiful in that dress at our wedding."

"Wow, I would have never guessed that yesterday when the two of you walked in here. I wish the best to both of you. I'd better go see if the cook can get this ready for a wedding dinner."

A while later, that most beautiful girl came walking through the door. The waitress ran over to her and said, "Wow, what a beautiful bride you are. I wish you would have come in wearing that dress from that lady's school in Boston. Come on over to sit with your husband. I'm so happy for the two of you."

Trinn looked at Tommy and said, "Did you have to tell the whole world we got married today? It's all right. I want the whole world to know you are my man. I plan on keeping you that way."

Their chicken dinner came through the door on a large platter. The owner of the Stockman's cafe came out behind the meal and asked what they would like to drink. "We have anything you want."

Trinn looked at Tommy and said, "A large glass of milk."

He grinned and said, "And what would you like, sir?"

Tommy looked around then looked at him, "I guess I have never been called sir. I'll have the same."

He again said, "I heard you just got married. Is there anything special you would like? We are here to make you happy. I hear that you, young lady, went to the lady's school in Boston."

"I think that the chicken dinner will be fine. In the camps where I was raised, they often had rattlesnake for their wedding dinners."

He again looked at Tommy and asked, "Where were you raised? I can't believe someone ate rattlesnake for a wedding feast."

Trinn said, "I did attend the lady's school in Boston, and Tommy here grew up and was raised as an Apache chief's son."

He looked at them once more and turned and walked back into the other room.

The waitress was standing there watching the events that just took place. She started laughing until tears came down her face. She pointed toward the owner. Then she broke into a laugh again. She then said, "That is the first time I've ever seen him not have something to say."

After eating and enjoying the fried chicken and the peas and potatoes and gravy, the waitress brought out a hot piece of apple pie. When she handed them the pie, she broke out into a laugh again. Trinn then broke into a laugh.

When they finished the pie, the waitress brought the ticket. Trinn looked at it. Reaching into her pocket to get the money for the meal, she stopped and said, "Oh, no! I forgot my money in my dress pocket."

Tommy jumped up and said, "I'll go get it. Is the key with you, or is it with the clerk?"

"It's hanging on the wall behind the desk in the lobby. Thank you for going and getting it. I love you, Tommy Quinn."

He looked back and said, "I'll be back if I don't get lost in the dark. I love you too, Trinn Quinn."

He headed down the boardwalk to the hotel. There was a walkway between the hotel and the Stockman's Café. As Tommy walked by the walkway, a club hit him in the back of the head.

Con and Mel grabbed him by the shoulders and dragged him to the alley. They had him over a horse and tied down in three minutes. They stayed to the back alleys and headed out of town for the barn where they had been staying.

After a half hour, Trinn began to worry about Tommy. The sheriff walked in for his supper, and the waitress ran over and grabbed him by the arm. She led him over to the table where Trinn sat, worrying.

He said, "What's wrong, Trinn?"

"Tommy went to our hotel room to get the money to pay for our supper. He never came back. Could you go with me to look for him?"

They walked into the lobby of the hotel and went to the front desk. Sheriff Howard asked the clerk if Tommy came and got the key to his room.

He looked at the board and saw the key to room 203 was still hanging on the wall. "I see the key is still there. I haven't seen him here since early this afternoon with this lady here. She came in earlier and changed out of that beautiful dress she was wearing. I don't think he has been here."

The sheriff said, "Give me the key, and we will go check it out."

Trinn walked in and looked around, "This room looks just like I left it earlier. Here is the money in the pocket of my dress. Here is the twenty-dollar gold piece Bill Wilson gave us for a wedding present."

"Let's go check the livery stable and see if his horse is still here. There has to be a clue somewhere. Someone had to see or hear something."

Brian, at the livery stable, said, "A cowboy came in looking for his horse earlier. He thought that it might have gotten loose, and somebody might have turned him in here. But I haven't seen that horse or that young man that was with this young lady here yesterday."

Trinn said, "Oh, I forgot to go back and pay for our meal. I had better go see if they are open."

The sheriff said, "They will be closed by now. You don't have to worry about the meal. I'll go in the morning and pay for the meal. Let's say as my wedding gift."

Trinn broke down, crying. She sat down right in the middle of the street and cried. "How can I go on without him? I just have to find him."

Sheriff Howard helped her to her feet and started walking to the hotel. When she was sitting on her bed in her room, he told her he would walk through the town and see what he could come up with.

# CHAPTER TWENTY-ONE

Con and Mel were heading for their horses behind the hotel when a man walked up beside them, leading his horse and asked, "What's going on here?"

Mel stepped in behind the man and lay his pistol behind the man's ear. He went down. Mel said, "Hurry, let's get him on his horse. We have to get out of town before someone sees us."

In three hours, they pulled up to the old homestead. "Let's get them into the barn. I don't believe anyone saw us leave town," Con said.

Mel said, "Why don't I find that lantern and get us a light so we can see where we are going? It would be a shame to fall and break a leg. It might be hard to get away. I'll get it."

With the lantern giving off some light, they led the horses next to the barn. They untied the unknown cowboy and threw him onto the hay. Mel said, "I guess he gets to sleep on our bed. It's been pretty soft. Kind of like a good hotel bed that we didn't have to pay for."

Mel untied Tommy from the saddle. He got hold of his shirt sleeve to pull him off. The sleeve tore off. He tossed it aside. "Too bad, it looked like a new shirt. Don't make them like they used to."

Con snorted, "We finally took care of him. He has been a headache to me since last spring. He gave me that ride into New Mexico across my saddle. I just returned the favor." He let out a loud laugh.

Mel looked around and said, "Why don't we put him over by that old wagon on the ground? We sure don't want to give him too soft a bed for his last night's sleep."

Con agreed then said, "We will take these horses with us. We can make a lot better time leaving this country. We need to head north toward Montana and get that Bill Wilson that shot up our friends."

Mel took the lantern and threw it against a post by the stall. The lantern fuel flew over the hay on the floor, instantly catching everything on fire.

"We need to make tracks as fast as we can out of this country."

Four hours later, they were several miles from the burning barn.

"Con, did you see how high those flames went? It sure was pretty. We will never have to put up with Tommy Quinn again."

Con smiled and let out another laugh. "I have wanted to do that to Quinn for months. He is dead and gone."

It started pouring down rain. An hour later, Con said, "Mel, quit complaining about the rain. It's washing away our tracks, so no one can follow us."

*****

Trinn had cried all night. She finally got off her bed. She talked out loud, "Where could Tommy have gone? I know he didn't just take off. I've got to find him."

Getting dressed in her riding clothes, she made sure she had her money this time. Taking her brush, she sat down on the bed to think. While doing so, she brushed her long red hair. She would brush it for Tommy Quinn. She pulled a few long red hairs out of the brush. *Red,* she thought, *like the Indians.* Then she started crying with the tears pouring down her face.

Up and heading for the sheriff's office, she started to get soaked from the rain. She knocked on the door then just walked on in.

Sheriff Howard sat on his chair. His eyes looked as if he hadn't had any sleep. "Have you come up with any clues as to where Tommy is at?" she asked.

"Trinn, I have walked this town from one end to the other almost all night long. I don't have a clue where he is at. I have this feeling that the Wadez brothers have something to do with it. I finally came in out of the rain. All tracks will be washed out. I am lost."

She sat down on the bench across from him. "I just don't know where to start looking. I may be that Apache kid's wife, but there is not enough Indian in me to track him down."

"I don't know what to say. The same day you get married, and you lose him. I'm buying breakfast if you have an appetite. Maybe we can think better with food in our bellies."

Walking into the Stockman's Café, they met the same waitress that had laughed at her boss the night before. She wasn't laughing. She had tears running down her face this morning.

Sheriff Howard looked at her then looked around to the empty tables. She came over and put her arms around Trinn's neck. "I'm so sorry for what has happened to you and that nice young man you married." At that, both of them began crying so much harder.

The sheriff took them both by the arms and led them over to the corner table where he usually sat when he ate his meals here.

The waitress looked up at him and said, "I guess you both came in to eat. I'm not being a very good waitress this morning. What would you like to eat?"

Trinn said, "I don't feel like eating. I just sat and cried all night. I guess I just want to sit and cry all day."

The waitress said, "I guess I would just like to sit and cry with you all day too."

Sheriff Howard had a couple of tears running down his face as well. Then he said, "I just wish I knew where those two dirty-faced Wadez brothers were. I'm sure if I found them, I would find Tommy."

At that point in the discussion, the waitress sat back and took a napkin from the table and wiped her face. "I know where they are. I know where Tommy is at. I'm not sure he is alive."

Sheriff Howard looked up at her and said, "How would you know that?"

"A couple of days ago, the day Tommy and Trinn came into town, those men came in late that night. It was just before closing. I made a comment about how dirty they were like they had been on a trail drive. They said they weren't but were waiting for the trail drive they had heard that was about to show up. I gave them some of the last of the stew and some coffee. I sat here at this table, and they were two tables down. I was just waiting for them to finish so I could lock up. I was listening to what they were saying."

Trinn took her by the arm and asked, "What did they say?"

"One of the men said, 'We have to stay out of sight. We need to get that Indian lover that rides with the herd.' The other said, 'What do we do with him? We can't take care of him in town?' The other answered, 'We'll take him to that abandoned barn we've been waiting in east of here. Then we'll cook him. Nobody will miss him or that old barn.'"

The waitress looked at Trinn and said, "That is all I remember. I wish I knew more."

Sheriff Howard said, "I know where that barn is. I'll ride out and check it out."

Trinn said, "I'm going with you. Let's get something fast to eat and go find out."

The waitress jumped up and headed for the kitchen. "I'll go get some ham and eggs on the skillet. The cook just took some hot bread out of the oven when you walked in."

She brought the sheriff a cup of hot coffee and Trinn a large glass of milk.

The sheriff said, "You can put that wedding celebration dinner on my tab. I guess I'm buying this morning too."

An hour later, they had their rain gear on and heading east. When they rode over the hill, Sheriff Howard pointed down to the barn. "Let's go see what we can find."

"I'm not so sure I want to go look, but I guess I need to know."

Riding up to the pile of ashes, Trinn looked down and saw a piece of cloth. She jumped off and picked it up. She recognized the sleeve and broke into tears again. "It's his sleeve," she cried. "I recognize it off the new shirt I bought him."

Sheriff Howard walked through the ashes. Then he noticed the body. The clothes were burnt off, and it turned his stomach to look at the body. He turned and walked over to Trinn and took her by the arm. "We need to get back to town. I'll send the coroner out to pick up the body. You don't want to see it."

She grabbed the sleeve and held it to her breast. "What will I do? I don't want to go on. I can't live without Tommy Quinn in my life!" she screamed.

The coroner brought the body in under a tarp. They found no bullet holes, but he had a broken skull. He asked the sheriff what Mrs. Quinn wanted to do with him.

She said, "I guess we can bury him here in Cheyenne."

Sheriff Howard had been doing some checking on the rewards of the three men. The State of Texas agreed to pay three thousand more. The town of Cheyenne agreed to pay for the burial of Tommy. The sheriff asked, "Should I have the money sent to the bank in Lander?"

"I'll take a hundred to cover my expenses here in Cheyenne. I haven't decided if I will ride and catch up with the herd or get a ticket on a stage and head to Lander," she said. "Maybe I'll just stay here in Cheyenne for a while. The doctor offered me a job."

Sheriff Howard wired US Deputy Marshal Noon in Abilene, Texas, to notify Quinn's family of his death.

US Deputy Marshal Don Noon,

This is to notify you that a young man named Tommy Quinn was murdered in Cheyenne, Wyoming. His wife, Trinn Quinn, asked me to notify you. He was married the same day. He was believed to be murdered by two men named Con Wadez and Mel Wadez. You had notified me that they were headed for Cheyenne. I looked for them but never located them. I'm not sure where they are now. Please let the Yost family know of his death. Also, let Sally Yost know and his brother Billy Quinn know.

Sheriff Lynn Howard of Cheyenne,
Wyoming.

# CHAPTER TWENTY-TWO

Things were going good for Bill Wilson. He was riding his horse part of the time. He had hired two more cowboys that knew the cow trails and waterholes on the way to Lander. They were brothers and had helped trail cattle from Lander to the railhead in Cheyenne.

In about twenty more days, he would be in Lander. Getting rid of half the cattle would make it a lot easier on him and the men. Some of the men were anxious to head back to Texas. Three of them had families.

Bill was sitting on the chuck wagon with Cookie. His thoughts were on Tommy and Trinn. Why hadn't they caught up with him? *I sure miss that boy. I guess that girl also.* They were like his children to him. The sheriff had said something about Con Wadez. Could he be the reason Tommy wasn't here?

"Cookie, what do you want to do when we get these cattle all delivered? You know, do you want to go back to Texas and keep doing this another year?" Bill asked.

"Well, boss, I guess Cookie might just stay where cows do."

Bill looked over and again asked, "You mean you want to stay in Wyoming out, wandering around in the hills?"

"No, boss. I get a job cooking on ranch. I have house to live in and family to be a part of. Maybe they even have big kitchen with a lot of pots and pans, maybe big cookstove. I cook them lot of apple pies. Maybe you go to work for them, and I cook you apple pies. Maybe I have kitchen of my own."

Lynn Bakken came riding up beside the chuck wagon. "Bill, we are coming up to the Chugwater Creek. It's getting late in the day.

Your new hand wondered if you would like to let the cattle rest and drink this evening. There is pretty good grass along the creek."

"If they think that would be best, let's do it."

Cookie said, "I sure miss Tommy. He always knows what is going on for several days ahead and behind at the same time. He always right. I miss that nurse of yours also. I think all crew miss her."

"I keep wondering why they never caught up with us. I am starting to worry if something happened to them. It just isn't like that Apache to not do what he says. We had better start keeping our eyes open for trouble. It must be about time for it to show up again," Bill said.

\*\*\*\*\*

Don Noon got the wire from Cheyenne that read:

US Deputy Marshal Don Noon,

This is to notify you that a young man named Tommy Quinn was murdered in Cheyenne, Wyoming. His wife, Trinn Quinn, asked me to notify you. He was married the same day. He was believed to be murdered by two men named Con Wadez and Mel Wadez. You had notified me that they were headed for Cheyenne. I looked for them but never located them. I'm not sure where they are now. Please let the Yost family know of his death. Also, let Sally Yost know and his brother Billy Quinn know.

Sheriff Lynn Howard of Cheyenne,
Wyoming.

He looked at it for the third time. A tear trickled down one cheek. How was he going to go face Bob Yost? What was he going to say? How was he going to face Sally? How was he going to face up

111

to Bob's wife? How was he going to face Billy Quinn that found his brother after all these years and wasn't going to get to see him? How was he going to face himself for a long time for letting that man out of his jail?

Tomorrow morning wasn't going to be good. Heck, all tomorrow wasn't going to be a good day at all. He walked over to the café and had them fix him a sandwich to take along. He wanted to get out of town before daylight.

This morning was going to be one of the longest rides of his life. He didn't want to face that family. Facing a half dozen blazing guns might be easier than facing what he had to do today.

He then thought of the thoughts he had a while back about that redhead that he would like to have a family with. How would he feel if a US deputy marshal rode in one morning when the sun was coming up on a beautiful day and he handed me that wire? The worst wire of his life. His son.

Tommy wasn't just a son to them. Noon felt the closeness deep in his chest for that boy. You had to just want him to be like the son you always wanted. Anyone that was around that boy had to want him to be their son.

He started to think of what did it say. He had to dig that wire out again. He pulled his horse up and got the wire out of his pocket. Those words just hit him. How did he miss them? He fumbled his hands, and they were shaking. He had to read them again to see if his mind was playing tricks on him.

His wife, Trinn Quinn, asked me to notify you.
He was married the same day.

It was there. How did he miss that? *His wife.* Somehow, it was on her wedding day. How did she feel? How could she go on? What kind of girl must she be to have him marry her when he had a girl like Sally wanting to marry him?

Tears started rolling down his cheeks. He thought about just turning his horse around and never coming back. How was he going to face Sally? How could he help the tears on Trinn's face that he knew had to be flowing? How was he going to help the tears of this whole family this day?

How was he going to stop his tears long enough to face them? How could he face Billy?

*Ride on great Texas Ranger. Ride on great US Deputy Marshal Noon.* That is what he must do to face up to his calling—face up to that name and the badge, the name "Noon" on that badge.

He rode down the hill toward the house. He could see Sally out doing chores. She was singing some kind of love song. He heard the name "Tommy Quinn" that had been placed in the lyrics of the song. She wasn't making this any easier.

She waved at him as he rode up. "You must have come for breakfast. Mom made biscuits and gravy. Come on in. The coffee is on the fire."

Bob Yost heard the voices and came out to see who was here. "Hello, Don. You must have come out to cheer us up and tell us some good news. Come on in. Breakfast is on the table."

Don rode over to the corral and tied his horse. As he was walking back to the house, his insides started turning.

Bob's wife had him sit on the end opposite of Bob. "Let's eat before you tell us why you rode clear out here."

He thought, *What a good idea.*

As he finished the third biscuit, he looked up and started crying. He tried to talk but couldn't.

Sally said, "It can't be that bad, can it?"

Don nodded then reached into his pocket and got up and walked to the other end of the table. He handed the wire to Bob. He turned and walked to the other end and sat back down. He put his head in his hands and started crying even harder.

He then took a deep breath. "I guess you had better read this. I sure had a hard time riding out here this morning."

Bob handed it to his wife. "You read it. I can't think that there would be anything in that that would make a strong marshal cry."

She opened the envelope and read the wire—word for word slowly with tears running down her face.

US Deputy Marshal Don Noon,

This is to notify you that a young man named
Tommy Quinn was murdered in Cheyenne,
Wyoming. His wife, Trinn Quinn, asked me to
notify you. He was married the same day. He
was believed to be murdered by two men named
Con Wadez and Mel Wadez. You had notified me
that they were headed for Cheyenne. I looked for
them but never located them. I'm not sure where
they are now. Please let the Yost family know
of his death. Also, let Sally Yost know and his
brother Billy Quinn know.

Sheriff Lynn Howard of Cheyenne,
Wyoming.

Tears were flowing all around the table. Sally got up and walked
over by Don. He stood up, and she wrapped her arms around him.
Don said, "I would have rather faced a half dozen blazing guns than
bringing you that wire this morning."

Mrs. Yost said slowly, repeating part of the wire, "His wife,
Trinn Quinn, asked me to notify you. He was married the same day."

Sally let go of Don and turned and said, "What did you just
say?"

Her mother repeated it. Then she said, "I wonder what kind of
woman this Trinn is that Tommy would marry her on a trail drive
halfway to Montana?"

Billy just sat there in shock. Sally came over to him and put her
arm around him. "I'm so sorry for you. I guess I forgot that you have
lost maybe more than any of us. You came all this way to find your
brother. Now you will never have that chance."

Billy replied, "Maybe it was worth the trip, just getting to
know you, Sally, and the rest of your family. You have all become my
family."

Then Mrs. Yost started crying again. "And I was the one that talked you into turning those men loose. It's all my fault."

Don cut her off, "I'm the one that made that choice. I opened the cell door. And if I hadn't, Sally and Billy might have been dead. You gave me reasons why I should do that to save these two. I had the final decision on the matter, and I'll live with it."

Sally looked at Billy and said, "I suppose that you will want to go back to Arizona?"

"As of right now, I want to stay with you and your family. I need your strength to carry me through this. You are such a wonderful family. I hope you don't mind if I stay for a while?"

Sally put her arms around him again and held him close. "I want you to stay as long as you want."

# CHAPTER TWENTY-THREE

*W*hat would Tommy Quinn do if he were here? What would Tommy Quinn want his wife to do? What do I want to do?

Trinn Quinn was still Tommy Quinn's wife, even if he was dead. *I will always want to carry that name. I will always love him. I want to know what my dad will think of me when he finds out that I left that lady's school he sent me to and paid for. I want to know what he will think of his little lady when he finds out that she married an Apache kid. I want him to love me. Most of all, find out what kind of person I really want to become. What kind of person am I way down deep in my soul? I* guess as she sat, thinking out loud, *I want this little "lady" to go help trail those cows to Lander. Then you better get out of bed, Trinn Quinn, and get some breakfast and supplies. Let Sheriff Howard know you are leaving. Get on that horse and head for home and Lander. Go get those questions answered.*

The sun was coming up, and she grabbed her clothes and put them in her bag. She walked down to the lobby and paid for her room. Breakfast was next. No, seeing the sheriff was next.

Walking across the street, she knocked on his office door. It came open suddenly. Sheriff Howard stepped back and said, "It looks like you're packed and ready to go somewhere."

She said with a determined smile, "I am going to go catch that cattle drive. I'm going to go and do what Tommy Quinn and I started. And I'm going home and see if my dad still loves me."

"That looks like you are leaving Cheyenne. Can I buy you one more breakfast at the Stockman's Café?" he asked.

She nodded and turned out the door, meanwhile grabbing his arm and letting him escort her back across the street.

She looked up at the little waitress who had cared so much and said, "I would like your eggs and biscuits and gravy. I want you to fix me a lunch for the trail."

The sheriff nodded a yes when the waitress asked him if he wanted the same. "It sounds like you've made up your mind that you are leaving us." She went in and ordered the breakfast and brought out a large glass of milk and a cup of coffee.

She sat down beside Trinn and reached over and gave her a hug. "I will miss you. I remember the first time you walked through that door. I'll hope I never judge you again like that. Where have you decided to go?"

"I'm getting on that horse of mine and going to go find that cattle drive. I'm going to go find out where the rest of my life is going to lead me."

The waitress went and got their breakfast and placed it on the table. "You have more inside you than I would have."

"I guess I need to go follow 'the Apache trail' wherever it leads me," Trinn said.

The sheriff walked her over to the store and picked up a few things for her to eat along the way. They headed for the livery stable. Brian was there putting shoes on a horse.

She walked back and got her horse and saddled him. She looked at Tommy's saddle and took his bedroll that she had held him under so close to her and put it on her saddle.

She asked Brian, "Would you keep Tommy's horse and saddle for a few weeks. I'll let you know what I want you to do with him. I'll pay you for the care of the horses now."

"I'll let you do that but only at half price. The rest will be your wedding present. I know that that might sound silly, but I just would like to help you somehow," Brian said. "I'll take care of his horse until I hear from you."

She had all her things tied on already. She turned and gave Brian a hug and a thank you. Sheriff Howard walked out in front of the stable. As he turned to bid her farewell, she gave him a big hug and a kiss on the cheek. "Thank you for all you have done for me."

She stepped onto her horse and gave him a wave goodbye.

*****

Con and Mel Wadez had been traveling for three days. Getting away from that barn and Cheyenne was a big concern. Now their concern was to find that herd and Bill Wilson.

Con said, "We haven't cut that trail drive yet. I wonder if they held up in Cheyenne or went another way. I guess we have to work our way back and find out."

Mel cut in, "Maybe we just need to head to California like that Quinn offered you a chance to one time."

"Don't you ever get it through your head? We are going after Wilson. Didn't you notice we took care of that Apache kid, Tommy Quinn? He didn't really have nine cat lives. If he did, we took care of the ninth one. He is dead unless he could get up and walk through the fire like they did in the Bible."

Mel said, "I'll bet that is the first time you ever referred to the Bible in your life. Mom tried to teach us, but we sure didn't listen much. Least we didn't follow much. I think we are probably guilty of murder."

"Why don't you just keep your mouth shut unless you can tell me where those cattle are. A thousand head of cattle has to leave some tracks. Let's go find them."

*****

Sam Perkins walked into the Bank of Lander to borrow some money to help pay his hands their monthly wages. Things were somewhat tight, at least until he could sell his yearling steers come fall. That was only a few months away.

As Sam got up to leave, the banker asked, "How's that daughter you sent back to Boston?"

"I hope she is becoming a lady. I sent her back there because she wanted to just be a cowboy here. She wanted to ride horses and work cows. She even broke several horses. Trouble was, she could outdo any of my men. Maybe she will find some banker back east and live a different life."

"I was just wondering why you had to borrow money from me when she has just put over thirteen thousand in a savings account for her in my bank."

Sam looked at the banker in disbelief and said, "You must be kidding me. Where would she have gotten that much money?"

The banker said, "It was wired into the bank in two different times this past week from a bank in Cheyenne. I guess that means she didn't rob it. Maybe she married that rich banker, and he plans on coming to Lander."

Sam sat back down across from the banker and looked dumbfounded. "I just don't understand. She is back in Boston, becoming a lady. I guess I could wire the bank in Cheyenne and find out about what is going on."

"They might not tell you much. We are not supposed to talk about other peoples' business. But I was curious to know why you were borrowing money with her having enough to buy you out."

"I'm worth more than that, but it would get a big part of it," Sam said. "I guess I had better find out who likes her that much."

The wire from the bank in Cheyenne was short and to the point.

To Sam Perkins:

Her husband had it sent into her account in Lander at her request.

Cheyenne

He thought he didn't know what was going on before. Now he knew that he knew even less. Her husband?

He was shaking his head as he walked up to his horse. What kind of lady has she become?

# CHAPTER TWENTY-FOUR

He had felt the heat scalding his back. He started for the door. There was enough light that he could see it through the smoke. He wasn't sure where he was. He wasn't sure about anything.

The heat was building, and he had to get away. He kept crawling until it became cooler. The coolness of the night. How did he get here? Who brought him here?

How his head hurt. His back was on fire. He crawled a little more to get away from the fire then passed out.

It felt good on his back. He turned over, and as his back sank into the mud, it helped the fire go out. It was pouring onto his face. He realized he was thirsty. He looked around and saw a water puddle. It was a little muddy, but it was wet. He crawled over to it and started to drink. Then he passed out.

He gagged and coughed the water out of his lungs. Carefully, he put his arm below his face. If he passed out now, his face would not be underwater. He got a good fill of water. He then tried to get up on his knees, and then he was on his feet. His head was going in circles. Staggering, he went on up the hill and over it.

Where was he going, he wasn't sure—away from the fire, back to. He wasn't sure where to. Then he passed out again.

The sun was up, and it was overhead. Then it was night again. What was he going to do? Then it was light again. He sat up and looked around. He had no idea where he was at.

Maybe if he went down by the fire, he could see some tracks to guide him, guide him to somewhere. He got to the pile of ashes. There were buggy tracks in the mud. They were a day old, but he had something to follow. He started to walk then passed out again.

When he woke, his face was next to a mudhole. He drank his fill. If only he had something to eat. It was dark. He turned over and put his back in the mudhole. That felt better.

Morning of another day had come, or had it been three or four days? He wasn't sure. He had to get back to his horse. Where was his horse? He got up and walked slowly. Where was he going? He wasn't sure yet, but it was starting to come.

He walked until he was exhausted. He sat down and went to sleep for a while. When he woke up, things were a lot clearer. He had to get back to town and his horse—his horse and the cattle. What had become of the cattle?

When he woke again, it was only a short distance from town. He got up and was doing a lot better this time, but he was so weak from not having anything to eat for days.

He walked down the street of Cheyenne and saw the sign of the Stockman's Café. He worked his way onto the boardwalk and through the door.

The waitress screamed as she saw the man covered with mud stumble in. She got a couple of men to help him into the chair at her table in the corner. There was blood running down from the top of his head. His back was bleeding.

She shouted, "Someone go get the doctor!" She lifted his head up and recognized that face. She screamed again, "Someone go get Sheriff Howard and fast!"

Tommy looked up and mumbled, "I need some food and water." Then he laid his head back on the table.

She went in and grabbed some stew and brought it back, along with a warm wet cloth to wash his face. Getting his face washed, she held his head against her shoulder and started feeding him the stew a little at a time.

After several bites, he tried to sit up. He finally made it and took the spoon and finished it. Sheriff Howard came running through the door. He couldn't believe what he was looking at. He had buried Tommy Quinn, and here he was looking at him straight in the face.

"I've heard that Apaches could live through about anything. Now I guess I will believe it. Tommy, who did this to you?"

Tommy raised his head and looked at him and said, "I have no idea, sheriff. I remember crawling out of that fire. It has taken me forever to get to town. I would like some of that milk and some more food."

As he had said the word milk, he remembered Trinn and getting married. They had milk for their wedding dinner.

"Where is she? I need my wife. She needs to fix my back. It hurts something awful."

Sheriff Howard said, "She took off for the cattle drive this morning."

Tommy started to get up. The sheriff pushed him back, "You need to eat the rest of your meal and that large glass of milk she's bringing you."

The doctor came through the door, saying, "I don't believe that it is him. We buried him yesterday." Looking up, he stopped in his tracks and took a deep breath. "Then, sheriff, who was that we buried in the cemetery yesterday? Let's take a look at you, young man. I guess when you get through eating, let's take you down to my office and clean you up. Then I can see you and doctor you."

Sheriff Howard started around to the bars and stores, asking if anyone knew who had come up missing the last few days. He then thought of seeing Tommy with a shirt with no sleeve. He was going past the mercantile and went in to find Tommy a new shirt. He found one the same color as the one he had on.

The doctor had Tommy cleaned up by the time the sheriff showed up. The doctor had found an old pair of blue jeans that were a might short but would work until the others got through the wash.

"You are one lucky young man to not get burned worse than you did. There are only a couple of bad burns into the skin. The rest will heal with only a little salve put on once or twice a day. Those two places lower on your back may need salve four times a day. That is quite a knife you carry on your back."

Sheriff Howard commented, "I noticed you don't wear a gun. Are you as good with that as Trinn told me you were?"

He looked up at the sheriff's eyes and said, "Probably faster when I'm putting it into a man. She has only seen me kill a turkey at thirty feet. We had a good dinner that night."

"I bought you a new shirt. The other one doesn't have a sleeve. The other sleeve was outside the burnt barn on the ground. Trinn found it. That is why she thought it was you in the barn dead. The last time I saw that sleeve was wrapped up in her arms like she was holding you in her arms like she never wanted to turn loose of you. You know she loves you an awful lot."

Tommy tried it on. It was the same size as the other shirt Trinn had bought for him. "I guess I'll wash those pants and hang them out. By the time I leave town, they will be mostly dry."

The doctor said, "I think my nurse already washed the mud out of them. They are hanging out on the line out back. You mean you would wear them wet?"

"A lot of the time, I just take my boots off and jump into a creek, and we all get washed off together. That's the way I did it riding with the Apache growing up. I always got dry sooner or later."

The sheriff asked again, "Do you know who the man was in the barn?"

"Sheriff, I have no idea. I can't even remember who hit me. They got me from behind, and I was out until I crawled out of the fire."

Tommy looked at the doctor and told him thanks, "I guess I'll have to get you paid later. I think my wife took all my money."

The doctor smiled and said, "That's the way it usually is. The wives usually take care of all the money. Of course, they usually are the reason their men have money at the end of the day."

The sheriff turned and said, "Put it on my account. I might as well donate a little more for a wedding gift."

Tommy turned and said thanks. "I've got to find my horse and find that girl. Whoever hit me is still out there! She might be in danger."

Brian turned loose of the leg of the horse he was shoeing. It landed on his foot. "What the heck! Horse that hurt! I thought you were dead, kid. We buried you yesterday. Don't you remember? Sheriff, is this his ghost, or did you go dig him up?"

Sheriff Howard answered with a smile, "If he is a ghost, then your foot doesn't hurt. 'Cause ghosts don't weigh anything."

Tommy said, "This ghost needs to ride out of Cheyenne. But being that no one sees ghosts, they will just be seeing a horse walk out of town. This ghost needs to catch up with his wife and scare the heck out of her. But maybe that wouldn't be such a good idea. She might get scared and shoot me."

Brian said, "Your stable fee is paid for another week. But I only charged her half price. I guess the extra will cover the doctor fee on my big toe."

Tommy had the saddle on his horse in fifteen minutes. "Do you know where my bedroll is at?"

"Your pretty wife took it. She didn't think you needed it where you were at. I guess she could look in the future pretty good. She left your horse and saddle here for you," Brian said.

"Thank you for all you have done for us. If I ever get down to Cheyenne again, I'll stop and visit. Maybe you won't let the horse step on your foot next time."

Marshal started to laugh but thought better of it. "Goodbye, son. You take care of that girl for me. If you catch those two, do something to help them remember what an Apache does to their captives."

"I told them last time if I ever had to deal with them again, I would stake them across an anthill and cut their tongues out like the Indians did when I was raised as an Apache."

"I better get down to the doc's and get my wet pants to cool me off. Thanks, Sheriff Howard, for all you've done for me, and especially for Trinn."

He took one jump, and he was on his horse, heading down the street.

He rode like an Apache in a whirlwind. He needed to make up for the time that she had a lead on him. He would ride until it got too dark to see, and then he and his horse would get some rest. The moon would be up in late evening, and he could get a move up the trail to that girl.

\*\*\*\*\*

Trinn was riding late tonight. She had to catch up to the cattle. She didn't want to travel after dusk because the rain had washed a lot of the tracks out. A thousand head still left a lot of sign for her to follow.

Starting a fire in a grove of trees by the creek, she would stay warm in Tommy's bedroll. Maybe she could dream of sleeping beside him like before. Maybe she would just have nightmares of him being burnt in that barn. The tears started to flow. How would she ever make it without him?

It would be several days until she caught up with the herd. As she lay by the fire, she thought about the dark. What would Tommy Quinn do? He would put the fire out, or he would make it look like someone was in the bedroll then get back out of sight of the fire. She did both, put out the fire and moved back into the trees. She sat where she could watch and listen to her horse. She climbed up into the tree above him. To tell the truth, she was scared.

It was almost daylight when she heard a horse walking along. Her horse let out a nicker. She had forgotten to be where she could have stopped him. She watched the rider turn and ride toward her slowly. It was still a little dark to see the rider. The horse moved slowly toward her. What was she to do? She had her gun on her hip. She was tired and cold. How was she going to make it to the cattle?

"Hail the camp," the voice called. "Is it all right for me to come in? Trinn, is that you?"

*It couldn't be him. He is dead.* But still she said, "Tommy, is that you?"

"Yes, it is. I'm glad I caught up with you. I'll ride on in and help you down from that tree."

As she slid down into his arms, he wrapped his arms around her and held and embraced her for a long time with a long, lingering kiss.

"I thought that you were dead. We buried you two days ago. I knew it was you because I found the sleeve off your shirt. How did you survive?"

Tommy held her close. She slid her hands down his back and gave him another hug. He jumped and let out a small cry. "That hurt, Trinn," Tommy cried.

She said, "What did I do? Are you hurt?"

"My back was burnt in the fire. I have some blisters on my back. I have some salve. I'm supposed to put on it four times a day and two times on the rest where it wasn't burnt so bad. I didn't get it on there yesterday while riding down here. I couldn't reach it. I guess that is why I had to get to my nurse."

She started to undo the buttons on his shirt. He stepped back and said, "What are you doing?"

"I'm taking your shirt off so I can put that salve on. Are you embarrassed to have me see you? Well, if you are, you had better get used to having me seeing you that way. Now where is that salve?"

He turned and walked over to his horse and got the salve from the saddlebags. He reached up and jerked his saddle off. Walking back over to her, he said, "I think we could have a rest and eat some breakfast."

She started putting the salve on then stopped and said, "How can you stand these burns? They are bleeding and raw. I hope I don't hurt you putting this on."

He stood there erect as she continued putting the salve on the sores. "When I was being raised Apache, they would burn me with a burning stick to see if I was tough enough to become a warrior and earn the place in the tribe. I had to do that and other things to prove myself."

She said, "I feel so sorry for you. You have had such a rough life."

"Don't feel sorry for me. That is what has made me the man that I have become. That is why they would take me out in the desert and leave me for a month at a time. All I had was my knife and my mind to help make it through. That is why I am what I am."

"I hope you don't have to raise our sons that way. I would hope there is a better way," she said.

She then put her arms around his neck and gave him a big kiss and held him tight. Looking into his eyes, she asked, "Could you eat some breakfast? I'm hungry."

He put his shirt back on and gathered some dry wood. He had the fire going in a few minutes. She grabbed some ham out of her bag and took a willow and held it over the fire. When it was cooked enough, she grabbed a couple of rolls and offered him some.

He said, "Let's get a few hours' sleep, and then we can be off. I didn't get much sleep last night. I don't think you got any, or you would have fallen out of that tree. You'll have to practice being a bird if you are going to perch in the trees at night."

She laughed and gave him a smile. She went over and picked up his bedroll and asked, "You mind sleeping with me again?"

# CHAPTER TWENTY-FIVE

Billy and Sally had ridden into the hills to check the cattle. The grass was growing high with all the rain. The ponds had water. The draws had their holes filled also. The calves were doing fine. The trees had a lot of shade under them.

Billy and Sally sat, eating their sandwiches they had brought. Sally lay back with her eyes closed, enjoying the coolness of the shade. Billy sat against the trees with his eyes closed.

Blinking open, he saw her lying there. He carefully moved over and bent over her and placed a kiss on her lips. Her eyes blinked open. "What do you think you are doing, Billy Quinn?"

"I'm stealing a kiss from the most beautiful girl in the world. I caught you with your pretty eyes closed and decided to see what I could do about what I've wanted to do in a long time."

She smiled and said, "How about taking a chance on it when I have my eyes open? You might never know what will happen."

He reached down and put a longer kiss on her lips. She wrapped her arms around his neck and held him there.

She said, "I guess we had better go check some more of the cows. Thank you for that, Billy. I have wanted to do that for a long time."

Billy said, "I thought you didn't want to get involved with me. But with Tommy not here, I thought that you just might allow us to get to know each other. I have fallen in love with you, Sally. I remember that first hug you gave me when I came home with your dad. I gave you that hug back for me. Those kisses a few minutes ago were for you from me."

"I have fallen in love with you the first few times we rode together. I always loved Tommy too. I felt that if I fell in love with you, I would be betraying the friendship I had with him. When we got that wire, I felt so bad about Tommy dying. Then there was that one sentence, those words, *his wife*. That hurt me so much. I guess I have to look at it from a different view. He liked me. He never told me that he loved me."

He said, "I am so sorry that I didn't get to meet him. I found him and lost him again in a matter of no time. But I am glad he could fall in love with someone and marry her. She must be quite a girl—then for her to lose him on their wedding day. I think that it is about time for me to go home and help with the family business. I would like you to go back with me. We could ride the stage. I'll leave my horse here for now."

"Why would you want me to go with you?"

He looked her in the eyes and said, "Because I would like you to go home and meet my family. They need to hear from you what Tommy was like. They need to know the girl that saved his life when he was all shot up. You need to tell them what he was like, to tell them what kind of man he had become, why you are proud of him. I want you to go home with me because I love you, Sally Yost."

She looked him in the eye and said, "That could almost sound like you are asking me to marry you, Billy Quinn."

He took her in his arms, and their lips met once again. "If you would take it as a proposal, then it is."

Giving him another hug and a kiss, she said, "Yes, yes, yes, Billy Quinn. I would love to be your wife."

He said, "I guess we had better get home, and I will ask your dad if he will let me marry you."

She smiled and said, "We could go to your home so I could meet your family. I will want to come back here to get married. I know my mom will insist on that."

"I'll insist on that too."

\*\*\*\*\*

Con and Mel Wadez had to turn back toward Cheyenne. The cattle had not gone to Montana. Con was upset. "I just don't understand. I worked for Bill Wilson. Those thousand head of cattle were heading to Miles City, Montana. You don't just turn a herd of cattle to who knows where after you have trailed them a thousand miles."

Mel turned to Con. "You know, Con, now is just as good of a time to head to California as any. Tommy Quinn gave you that chance. We could have a good life. You got your revenge on him. I would like to just head west."

Con screamed at him, "If you want to head for California, then go! I don't consider you my brother if you turn and ride out on me. I don't need you to get Bill Wilson. Tommy Quinn is gone and dead. He was the only one that stood between Bill Wilson and me."

Mel pulled up his horse and studied what Con had just said. He turned his head toward California. "I wish you well. I need to go live my own life. I never want you controlling my life again."

"You are just a coward, Mel. I don't ever want to have anything to do with you again."

Mel just kept riding, raising his hand high in the air in a farewell wave.

Con was heading southwest when he ran into the cattle tracks. He turned and followed. He stopped in a small town. He inquired where the cattle herd was headed. The store owner said, "You are a few days behind the cattle. They are heading toward Casper. I heard they have half the herd sold in Lander to a rancher there."

He got some supplies and headed for Casper.

*****

Tommy and Trinn rode into Douglas. They asked about the herd of cattle that had come through the day before. "There was a man following that herd here this morning. I guess he wanted to hire on. Said the Boss was Bill Wilson."

Trinn got some matches and another blanket to go along with Tommy's bedroll. Tommy said, "We have to catch Con before he gets to the herd."

Walking out, they were on their horses and heading to Casper. If they pushed, they could catch up with Con.

Trinn pointed down into the trees and saw a campfire. They got close enough to see only one man in the camp. Tommy said, "We will get ahead far enough to catch Bill before he gets to them."

Trinn asked as Tommy rode through the night, "Don't you ever get tired? I am about ready to drop out of this saddle."

"We will go for about two more miles and stop and get some rest for a couple of hours. We have to be ahead of Con when he gets near the cattle herd."

Two days later, they caught up with the herd. The cattle were just past Casper. Tommy and Trinn scouted around town to see if any of Bill's crew were there. Con was on their tail and would be in Casper that evening.

They tied their horses out of sight. Slipping in the back door of the café, they got a fried chicken dinner with two large glasses of milk. Back into the ally, they watched for Con.

Looking up the boardwalk across from the sheriff's office, Bill was walking his way to the café down the street toward them. Looking the other way, he saw Con walking forty feet from him.

Con yelled at Bill, "You shot and killed my men. I have taken care of Tommy Quinn. Now you will die."

Tommy pushed Trinn back out of sight, then he stepped between Bill and Con. He was thirty feet from Con. "Con, I'm still alive, and I'm not wearing a gun. I was hired on to protect Bill Wilson. If you want Bill, you will have to go through me."

"Quinn, I killed you in Cheyenne. You're dead." He drew his gun. The knife stuck in his heart. Con looked at Tommy and said, "You didn't even…" Then he quit talking and fell over on his face.

The Sheriff Buck Stiffner walked over to Con and turned him over. "I had word from Sheriff Howard that Con had killed a man in Cheyenne. I guess you are Tommy Quinn that he tried to kill several times."

Bill walked up and looked at the man facing up. "I guess I can quit watching over my back. Let's go get something to eat, and you can tell me what you have been doing on your honeymoon."

Tommy said, "Trinn and I have already eaten the rest of our wedding dinner. I believe they had apple pie in the café. I didn't have time to eat it. I had to come and save your hide again. Let's go eat the pie you're going to buy for us while I tell you about that great honeymoon."

Two weeks later, they came in over the ridge, overlooking the Simons Ranch. The hands started cutting off the count of five hundred head of the cattle. They moved the balance on down the creek. They would hold the cattle there until Bill talked to Trace.

While the hands were doing the sorting, Trinn and Tommy rode five miles over to the Perkins Ranch. She walked up to the porch and knocked on the door. Sam opened the door to see his daughter and a stranger standing beside her. He just stood there, looking at her and not saying anything.

"Daddy, is it all right if I come in?"

He blinked his eyes and let out a breath. Then he stepped up to her and put his arms around her. "What are you doing here? I sent you to Boston to become a lady."

"Daddy, is it all right if I come home? I became all the lady I could stand. I worked my way home."

Sam said, "Why did you come home? I sent you to Boston."

She said, "Daddy, is it all right if I come home? Daddy, do you love me? I came home because this is my home, and I love you, Daddy."

"Who is this man that is with you? He looks like a saddle tramp you found along the trail."

She came back with "No, Daddy, he found me along the trail. I love him, and I married him. His name is Tommy Quinn, and my name is Trinn Quinn."

"Why did you come home? I wanted you to be a lady, my daughter."

Tommy said, "Sir, would you like Trinn and I to go and leave? If she isn't welcome, we will move on."

Sam said, "I didn't want my daughter to marry some no-account saddle tramp."

"You may want to know that I am not just any no-account saddle tramp. I was also raised by an Apache chief, even as his son. I was hired by Bill Wilson to follow along with his trail herd. I didn't really move the cows. I mostly just wandered around, watching the rest of the hands move the cows. I know how to be a savage. I killed a man last week in Casper. I guess I just married Trinn for her wealth. I love her, and she loves me. We will get off your ranch."

They both turned and walked out, heading into Lander.

*****

Bill had the cattle sorted. "I want to go see how my top hand and his wife are getting along. We will all meet Trace Carter in town in the morning and settle up with you and him and find out where we will take the other cattle. I'll stop at the Perkins Ranch and check on Trinn and Tommy. I'll ride on in and see you in the morning."

Knocking on the Perkins door, Bill introduced himself. "I wanted to make sure Trinn and Tommy got settled in all right."

Sam looked at him, "Are you another one of those saddle tramps? I sent my daughter down the road. He told me he was raised by the Apache, and he followed you from Texas. Not even helping move the cattle. He said he married my daughter for her money. I don't need a no-account saddle bum on my place. You can get your no-account hired help and leave my place." He then gave Bill a shove out the door.

Bill took one swing with his good arm and placed it in Sam's face. When he went down, he kicked him in the ribs with his good leg. When he went to get up, Bill kicked him in the jaw. "Now if you get up again, I'll knock you back down. You are going to lay right there and listen to me. I'm not a no-account hired hand. I hired Tommy Quinn to protect my hands and me clear from Texas. He did that better than any ten men could have. He fought men, and they tried to kill him. He crawled out of a burning barn and got back to Cheyenne. He took off that very day with blisters bleeding on his back to catch up with Trinn. He made it into Casper just in time to step in front of a man drawing to shoot me. He faced him with just

133

a knife and killed him. That no-account faced ten men that came to kill me. He took them on."

Sam said, "I didn't know."

"If I were you, I would lose my pride and beg their forgiveness. I would give my whole life to have him be my son and Trinn to be my daughter." Bill turned and walked out.

*****

Trace Carter met with Bill for breakfast in Lander the next morning. Trinn and Tommy were in the restaurant when Trace and Bill walked in. Bill walked over and introduced Trace to the young couple. The banker walked in and over to Trace. With all there, they ordered breakfast. Sim would be along soon. The banker said, "Sim has given me the go ahead to pay you and wire the money to your bank in Miles City. Bill, what do you need to be paid to date for what you've done?"

Bill told them what the hands needed as agreed. "The only thing here is I agreed to pay Tommy what he was worth to me. I thought about that price. He dealt with two groups several times that were going to kill the crew—also, with bands of Apache Indians several times. He was almost killed to save us and me several times. He got us across the river in time to save the whole herd."

He looked at Trace and the banker. "What is that worth? Not to say his wife doctored me back to health after a broken leg and arm. She also rode every day, moving the cattle alongside the men."

"Trace, are we taking the rest of the cattle to Warmwater? We are ready to go where you want."

Sam Perkins had been sitting with his back to the men. He had come in to see if he could find his daughter and ask her forgiveness. He had been listening to what was said about Trinn and Tommy. He got up and walked over to Trinn and Tommy. He then looked at Bill and said, "I owe all of you an apology. Bill, you knocked some sense into me. After listening to what kind of man my daughter married, I owe them an apology. Trinn, I do love you. I beg you to come home.

Tommy, there is room for you as part of the ranch. You two are equal partners with me."

They all sat, listening to Sam. Then they stood up and shook hands, and Sam asked forgiveness for breaking up their meeting.

Trace asked Sam, "Could you run more cattle on your place?"

Sam said, "Four hundred head."

"I need two hundred head taken over to Bill Snyder's ranch at Warmwater. He wants to have the cook stay and cook on the ranch. His wife got killed, and he wants a good cook."

Bill popped in and said, "We have the best cook in the world. He told me he was going to stay and move in where the last cows were sold." Bill looked around and asked, "What about the other three hundred head?"

"If Tommy could buy them from me, I'll sell them to him. I can't afford to just give them to him, but I'll take two thousand dollars and what he is worth to the outfit, which is probably more than the whole bunch."

Trace said, "If you can trail the rest to Warmwater, you can have half the check to pay for your hands and you. Bill, you can collect the money from Trinn and Tommy for paying for his cattle. You and I will split that money. Your half of that money is yours above your split of the Snyder money."

The banker cut in, "Trinn, the sheriff in Casper sent you a two thousand dollar reward for Con Wadez. How about I give this to Bill Wilson and Trace? You can consider the cows paid for."

"Tommy, I guess I owe you a lot," Bill said. "My life several times, the herd several times, your wife's nursing and helping herd the cattle as one of our best saddle tramps. We can make it on over to Warmwater without you. We will cut your three hundred head out and trail them over to the Quinn and Perkin's ranch. Sam, if you would let this Apache kid trail his cattle to your outfit, we will help him."

"I need to talk to Sam privately." Bill pulled Sam aside and said, "Sam, this young man was taken from a wagon train at six years old. He was raised as the Apache's chief's son for ten years. He was brought up by them. He was shot up on an Apache raid on a ranch in Abilene, Texas. The Yost family saved his life. His brother, Billy Quinn, came looking for him after he came to be my and my men's bodyguard. Tommy Quinn has never seen his brother or the rest of his family for over sixteen years. They thought he was dead. He thought that his family was killed in the Apache raid when he was six years old. He lived with the Yost family for six years. He is the best young man you could ever want for family. Your daughter loves him and you. I ask you one favor. Put them on a stage for Abilene, Texas, this week. Let him go meet his brother and his family. Let him meet the Yost family who thinks he was killed in Cheyenne. Thanks for what you did today. I would be proud for him to be my son. I will pay the stage ticket for them out of that money the banker just said he would give me."

# CHAPTER TWENTY-SIX

Sally and Billy got off the stage in Tucson, Arizona. They walked down to the wagon in front of the Quinn Freight Office. His mother looked up and let out a scream. She ran out to the street and gave her son a hug.

She then noticed Sally. "Who is this beautiful girl? Where did you find her?"

"This is Sally Yost from Abilene, Texas. She nursed Tommy back to health six years ago. Tommy lived with them until he took off to Montana on a trail drive. I guess there is something I have to tell you that I haven't had the nerve to. Tommy got married in Cheyenne, Wyoming. That same day, he was murdered."

His mother sat down on a box by a freight wagon. She started crying. "How can this happen to me? After all this time and we found him and lost him all at once."

Mr. Quinn came out of the back and saw his wife crying. He asked, "What is going on here?"

Billy said, "I caught up with Tommy. But he had taken off on a trail drive to Montana. He was supposed to be back by spring. He got married in Cheyenne, Wyoming. Then he was murdered the day of his wedding."

He sat down by his wife and put his arms around her. "Who is this girl?"

"I am Sally Yost from Texas. I nursed Tommy to health six years ago after he had been shot up in an Apache Indian raid on a ranch. He had been raised as an Apache Chief's son for ten years after he was taken from you. We taught him to read and write. He lived with us for six years. I came to tell you about him."

Mr. Quinn asked, "Why do bad things always happen to us? Tommy was just always in the wrong place."

Billy cut in, "He must have had some happiness in his life to get married."

"Marriage is surely a good thing, but why was he killed?" Mrs. Quinn asked.

Billy asked, "Mom and Dad, I need to ask you a question. Would you be willing to travel to Abilene, Texas, next month?"

"Why would we want to do that, son? We have a business to run."

"To be at Sally's and my wedding. We would like you to be there. I promised Sally's mom that we would come back there for the wedding," Billy said. "We would then come and help here with the business."

Mr. Quinn said, "We will work it out. We have to. My brother will just have to take care of the business."

*****

A month later, the Quinn family stepped down from the stage in Abilene. The Yost family met them at the stage office. The families were excited to see each other.

Sally asked, "Mom, have you got things arranged for the wedding?"

Mrs. Yost answered, "On Wednesday at 2 p.m., we will have it at the church. We brought the wagon so we can all ride out to the ranch together. I have to finish your dress."

"Let's go down to the café, and all get some dinner. Some of the neighbors and town people plan on a big dance and dinner after the wedding," said Mrs. Yost.

Sally was in her beautiful yellow dress. She was the best-dressed lady in the town. The Yost family came into town with the Quinn family. Mrs. Quinn said, "There is only one thing that would make this day better." Mrs. Yost agreed but said it could never happen. Mrs. Quinn said, "Only God could make it happen."

Sally said, "Mrs. Quinn, I have prayed for that every day all summer. I keep praying he does come. At least in spirit."

*****

The stage rolled in at one o'clock as scheduled. Trinn and Tommy stepped out of the stage. Trinn asked, "What is going on down at the church at the end of town? Looks like half the country is heading there."

Tommy said, "I hope it's not a funeral."

Trinn said, "It can't be. Everyone is dressed in bright colors. Maybe they are celebrating you coming home, Tommy Quinn, but I don't think they know that you were coming home."

As they walked through the door of the church, everyone quit talking. Tommy and Trinn looked at each other. Sally came running down the aisle, screaming, "Tommy Quinn is home!"

# ABOUT THE AUTHOR

Roy Schatz was born and raised on a cattle ranch near Meeteetse, Wyoming. He rode Wyoming hills and mountains chasing cattle, wild horses, wild buffalo, and breaking horses over the years. While taking care of a ranch in Jackson Hole, Wyoming, the Teton National Park service manager asked him to move herds of buffalo several times with his Appaloosa horse.

He graduated from the University of Wyoming in 1974 and married his wife, Kathy, that has inspired him over the years. They enjoyed their honeymoon riding horses, staying in a sheepherder's teepee tent with no heat in the middle of the winter in the deserts of northern Wyoming. He ranched for over forty-six years with his wife and children in northern Wyoming, except for when he and his wife served a full-time mission for the LDS church. He served in the armed service before he was married. He also drove truck for about five years over the road across Canada and throughout the continental United States, except Maine and Rhode Island.

Roy's grandfather's family move to the Indian nations of Oklahoma when his grandfather was three years old. His grandfather was raised in the Indian nations around the Apache. He went swimming with the Apache kids in Cash Creek northwest of Fort Sill, Oklahoma. In his life history, his grandfather talked about what Geronimo said to him. He knew him personally. His grandfather also met Buffalo Bill Cody several times, as well as, Annie Oakley. His grandfather taught Roy some things about the Apache. This included taking the hair off deer hides and making rawhide out of them, making arrow heads with a deer antler, and making bows from branches cedar trees. He would bury the branches in the mud of a pond over the winter so it would give the bows the spring to shoot arrows over eighty yards. His grandfather's mother was part Indian.

CPSIA information can be obtained
at www.ICGtesting.com
Printed in the USA
BVHW072230291021
620256BV00001B/7